Annie O'Neil spent most of her childhood with her leg draped over the family rocking chair and a book in her hand. Novels, baking, and writing too much teenage angst poetry ate up most of her youth. Now Annie splits her time between corralling her husband into helping her with their cows, baking, reading, barrel racing (not really!) and spending some very happy hours at her computer, writing.

THE PRINCESS
AND THE
PAEDIATRICIAN

ANNIE O'NEIL

MILLS & BOON

First published in Great Britain 2021
by Mills & Boon, an imprint of HarperCollins*Publishers* Ltd,
1 London Bridge Street, London, SE1 9GF

www.harpercollins.co.uk

HarperCollins*Publishers*
1st Floor, Watermarque Building,
Ringsend Road, Dublin 4, Ireland

Large Print edition 2022

The Princess and the Paediatrician © 2021 Harlequin Books S.A.

Special thanks and acknowledgement are given to Annie O'Neil
for her contribution to The Island Clinic miniseries.

ISBN: 978-0-263-29356-2

01/22

MIX
Paper from
responsible sources
FSC™ C007454

For tropical islands that pare us down
to our essence and let love bloom.
I know it sounds crazy, but I was
proposed to on a tropical island,
so I LOVE them and hope you do, too.

CHAPTER ONE

THOUGH LIA WOULD never admit it, there were some perks to being a princess.

'Champagne?' asked a passing waiter.

Flutes of fancy fizz when you were really, really nervous was one of them. If only it could make her feel as bubbly as it looked.

She scanned the room to see if she could catch a glimpse of her boss, Dr Nate Edwards, for a confidence-boost. She hadn't seen much of him around the clinic lately, so she'd thought perhaps they'd catch up tonight at the gala. She'd even shown up early, to check out all the donations from local businesses who seemed to have outdone themselves with their generosity of amazing-looking food, floral displays and just about everything in between for the silent auction.

She scanned the room again. Nope. No Nate. She was beginning to regret the effort she'd gone to with her 'princess' gear. Swishy dress. Actual make-up. Tiara.

Only her huge-hearted boss and a good cause like the St Victoria Foundation could get her to pull out her blow dryer and mascara wand, let alone the tiara. Otherwise she'd be parked in the corner of her extra-comfy cottage, wearing her softest cotton jim-jams and watching a box set.

But tonight the box set would have to wait. The Foundation was holding its annual charity gala, and guests hobnobbing with a princess helped boost the coffers. It didn't mean it made her any less socially awkward, though. Casual chit-chat was definitely not her forte.

She was about to accept a glass of fizz when she pictured the white-blonde, pinch-faced woman with a clipboard who attended official events with her back in Karolinska. She could practically see the woman wrinkling her nose, then hissing, 'Say *No, thank you*. And you've got lipstick on your teeth.'

The flipside of the perks.

The Princess Faux Pas Posse—or the PFPP as she called them—was a little tribe of helpers the palace back in Karolinska sent to babysit her on the rare occasions when she participated in an official event. They pointed out things like…oh, ketchup on her face, a bit of spinach in her teeth, or—the one the press hadn't let go of for ages—her hair blowing across her face so it looked as if she had a Victorian moustache.

This wasn't even her official event—it was Nate's. He was the founder of The Island Clinic here on St Victoria, her Caribbean home away from prison.

Home! She meant home away from *home. Obviously.* A palace was hardly a prison.

She sniggered. Try telling that to the Tower of London.

She gave her head a shake. She wasn't British, nor waiting to get her head chopped off by Henry VIII. And she'd left modern-day Karolinska, where royal traditions felt like medieval shackles, three years ago now. The warm nights and sea-salted air were regular reminders that she had changed her life to be precisely that. *Hers.* St Victoria spoke to her every bit as much as her homeland did.

Luckily, Karolinska had diplomatic ties with the government here and, unlike her homeland, St Victoria boasted a glorious tropical sprawl of warm beaches, an extraordinary medical clinic, and—more to the point—no PFPP.

Here, she felt able to breathe. She could work without worrying about being *'The Spinster Surgeon Princess'*, as she would no doubt be described in the headlines of the papers back home. She'd been every manner of princess— *single/alone/lonely/little*—since her parents had split. Now that she was in her early thirties she could add 'spinster' to the list.

Being labelled by the media was something she probably should've got over a million years ago, but…

It wasn't all bad, of course. Loath as she was to admit it, sometimes it was fun dressing up. And this was the one night of the year she went full-on glam. And who didn't like the swish of fabric against their legs when it had been…oh, about three years since they'd felt the touch of a man's hand?

She gave her head a short, sharp shake. Where had *that* come from? She was quite happy with her job and with being one hundred per cent in control of her life, thank you very much.

Well. Most of it. The palace was pretty good at tightening the noose when it wanted to.

She thanked the waiter but refused the drink. She was a representative of The Island Clinic tonight, and as such needed to keep her wits about her. She'd have a glass once the press had left and there was no danger of an 'incident' being reported back to the palace.

And by 'incident' she meant embarrassment. Members of the Karolinskan Royal Family did not embarrass The Crown. 'Twas ever thus.

Which, of course, brought out her mischievous side.

She pulled her mobile out of the delicately woven palm frond clutch one of her patients had given her and, after a surreptitious glance around, took a goofy selfie in front of an enormous floral display, which was designed to look like a tropical flower guide to the Caribbean Islands.

She tapped in her cousin's number. He had donated the special *grand cru* for this event. He was probably out on a peace-keeping mission with the rest of his squad. It was how Jonas spent most of his time these days—in wellworn army fatigues, keeping the peace in volatile hot spots in the world. Places she should be as well, providing medical care, but wasn't thanks to the King and Queen…aka Grand-mama and Grandpapa.

Yes, thanks to them, and to her father's inability to stand up to them on her behalf, instead of following up the years of military medical training she'd poured her heart and soul into with an appropriate career, she 'kept the peace' in a different way. Patient by patient, case by case, at The Island Clinic.

She'd been drawn to the clinic after reading about its extensive charitable work. And events like tonight's ball would help ensure the clinic could carry on with the promise that no patient in need of their elite treatment would be turned away. She genuinely loved it. She was a neurosurgeon, and there were some incredibly interesting cases which she never would've seen if she hadn't wrangled her way round the palace's rules and found this job.

Another one of the catering staff swept by, miraculously managing to balance a tray filled with sparkling glasses of fizz even as her hips moved to the rhythm of the guitarist who was warming up on the small stage.

The woman did a quick double-take when she

recognised Lia, and instantly swirled the tray round in front of her. 'Champagne?'

Lia flushed, as she usually did when she was recognised, and said, 'No, thank you.' Then, in a burst of spontaneity, she tapped the side of her nose and with a grin said, 'Not yet, anyway.'

The woman sashayed away with a knowing laugh.

Lia looked around the room and, as she was on her own, let herself have a sway to the music, too, crossing her arms so that one hand rested on each hip.

It really had been a long time since she'd been held by a man.

She pulled a face. Being horny was not usually her thing. Nor was it helping her align her focus to where it should be. On the guests about to arrive.

They were going to have such fun tonight. Beautiful music, amazing food—all supplied by talented and warm-hearted local businesses—and, thanks to the ballroom staff here at the Harbour Hotel, in an absolutely beautiful location. If ever there was a night to donate a million dollars to an excellent charity, or to…say… share a first kiss…this was it.

The event team had extended the sumptuous floral aesthetic of the loggia surrounding the sprawling hacienda-style building into the ballroom. All of the carved wooden sliding doors had been tucked away into invisible corners, so that the glittering harbour could be seen twinkling away. The arches soaring up to the double-height ceilings were hidden behind massive palms bearing swirls of fairy lights. The tables were dappled with beautifully perfumed flowers perched in cleverly crafted banana leaf 'vases'.

The overall effect was tropical chic at its finest. A true celebration of all that was beautiful on the island of St Victoria, and a reflection of the spirit of the community who lived on it. Generous, kind, gorgeous people Lia hoped she would never have to say goodbye to if—heaven forbid—duty ever called.

Speaking of which…

She tapped out a quick message to her cousin.

Hey, Jonas, what do you think of my island look? I'm sure our grandparents would love it! LOL. We're in the throes of the rainy season, but tonight it's dry and deliciously cool. For the

Caribbean, anyway. Still not worn a jumper. Has the snow started back home? Ha-ha. Kidding/not kidding. Enjoy your summer if you're home. Catch-up video-call soon? Lia x

Her thumb hovered over the 'send' button as she took a moment to examine the photo she'd just snapped. Her long, very Scandinavian-looking blonde hair was in a thick, loose plait, woven together at the back of her head with a smattering of the beautiful tropical flowers that bloomed here year-round. The delicate purple of the blossoms was a nice accent to the eggshell-blue maxi dress she'd decided to wear tonight. It managed to both look elegant and be comfortable—one of her prerequisites now that she was choosing her own outfits.

After years of being handed photos by the disappointed palace press secretary, who loved to point out how awkward and uncomfortable Lia looked, she'd finally asked for 'classy, but with room to breathe' to be the guideline for all the clothes designers sent to her.

It hadn't made much of a difference.

Moving countries had.

Since she'd moved here to St Vic, well out of

'lens shot' of the paparazzi, the designer clothes had dried up and—surprise, surprise—she'd begun to look less awkward and uncomfortable in the rare photos she appeared in. Clothing, she realised, had had nothing to do with her discomfort.

Smiling and looking pretty as a princess simply wasn't her thing.

Doing something that made a genuine difference was.

She felt her smile falter as she thought back to the days when, as only sixth in line to the throne, she'd never taken centre stage on the palace balcony family portraits, but had always been required to *be* there, waving, smiling, looking out over the fairy tale main square of the capital city of Karolinska and, more importantly, at the people who revered the royal family and all they stood for.

Stoicism. Duty. Scandinavian pride.

In fairness, her country *was* beautiful. Nestled between Sweden and Denmark, it was almost entirely comprised of little islands dotted about the Baltic Sea—except for the capital city which stood proudly on the mainland coast. A beacon of Scandinavian beauty and civic pride.

As a nation, they were highly regarded for their strong moral compass on matters of global import and for their generosity when it came to the social well-being of their citizens. As her grandfather the King often said, 'We set the standard the rest of the world must follow.'

She had a few rebuttal points for that, but... Loyalty, loyalty, loyalty! That was how it worked in her family.

She shivered as she felt the claws of family obligation dig deep into her core. How was it that they still held so much power over her, three years after she'd left the snow-capped rooftops of Karolinska behind?

She squinted at the photo, trying to divine if something—*anything*—had changed in her in the time since she'd arrived on the pristine white sandy beaches of St Victoria.

She blinked in surprise.

Gosh...

Three years of island life *had* changed her.

She looked happy. Genuinely happy. And why not? She was mostly free of the royal shackles that had weighed her down back home. The loneliness. The hunger for a so-called normal family. Well... Okay, so she was still lonely, and she was absolutely without a doubt single. And, judging by all her not entirely appropriatc thoughts she was a little bit lusty… But at least her grandmother wasn't trying to set her up with 'suitables', as she called them.

Here, Lia was on the periphery of a different type of family: The Island Clinic. It was a mismatch of international and local doctors and health professionals, brought together by the clinic's American founder Nate Edwards.

To the staff, she wasn't Princess Amelia Margit Sigrid Embla Trelleburg of Karolinska, sixth in line to the throne, as she was back in Europe. Here she was free to be plain old Lia. Or Dr Li-Li, as some of the nurses and patients called her.

Not that it happened that frequently… Being comfortable in her own skin was still something she was working on. As was trusting people to be her friend for no other reason than that they liked her. But she'd get there one day. So long as everyone who was in line to the throne before her stayed healthy and well. She *never* wanted to take The Crown. Managing her own life was hard enough, thank you very much.

Soon enough the room began to fill, and introductions came in a long stream of names she'd never remember. It was overwhelming, but all for a good cause.

As she eventually wended her way through the tables towards her own seat she fought the lonely feeling that inevitably began to hollow her out at big events like this. The tables were filled with people dressed in all of their finery, chatting away, laughing, smiling, listening. Oh, she could put on a show and do the same, but her childhood hadn't prepared her to feel at ease in a crowd...

A mother who'd hated the limelight, a father who'd bowed and acquiesced to the throne, and a shocking divorce had meant the palace had taken over the 'finer points' of her upbringing and given short shrift to that. One-on-one inter-actions were more her style. And even then...

She smiled and nodded, shook the odd hand, gradually feeling more and more isolated as she approached the head table where she guessed Nate wanted her—*still no Nate!*—and stood behind her chair.

Why did being in a crowd always feel like the loneliest place in the world?

She held back the inevitable grimace, weighted

with bad memories. There were a thousand reasons why and all of them had to do with growing up in her family. One that could've been happy if only—

She forced her thoughts to screech to a halt.

If only nothing. What was done was done. If she wanted to carry on being happy here on St Vic, she'd have to find a way to re-establish how she dealt with people. Just because her parents were divorced, and her mother had been ostracised, and Lia had been sent off to moulder away in a remarkably unpleasant convent school for the entirety of her childhood, didn't mean her adulthood had to be miserable. Just as she had the power to change someone's life in the operating theatre, she also had the power to change her own.

Having told herself off, she scanned the vast room and forced herself to think of all of these people as potential friends. Or... Her eyes skipped from one male face to another. Potential boyfriends? It was an area of her life she was particularly gun-shy about. The last few had wanted to live the life they'd thought royals led, only to discover it wasn't quite the way the society papers would have had them believe. Suffice it to say being dumped by text when you were a princess was a double blow.

There had been one name—well, a face, really—that had stood out from the crowd earlier. A paediatrician from the UK whose name she hadn't been able to catch, because before he'd got to her in the greeting queue he'd spotted a little boy who'd been treated at the clinic. He'd left the queue and shared a jolly greeting with the lad and his parents before the pair of them had completed a very intricate handshake only the two of them seemed to know.

She'd liked that. Honouring a child she presumed had been his patient over kowtowing to 'royalty'.

Well. Royalty. Without the quotes.

She was genuinely royal, whether she liked it or not.

Out of the corner of her eye she saw a rather lovely male hand take hold of the back of the chair next to hers. It looked strong, capable, and oddly callused for someone she presumed was a doctor.

'Is this seat taken?'

She was about to say yes, that they were all assigned seats, when she realised the very man she'd been thinking of was standing next to her. Tall. Athletically lean. Short caramel-blond hair. And piercing blue eyes that sparkled in the twilight hues of the ballroom lighting.

Unlike a lot of the guests who didn't seem able to look her directly in the eye—because of the princess thing—this man didn't seem the slightest bit intimidated. He had an aura of strength about him that spoke of a deep-seated kindness, an inner peace that didn't necessitate any shows of bravura or machismo.

She glanced down at the name card.

Oliver Bainbridge.

She surprised herself by fixing him with a cheeky grin. Something about him made her feel comfortable. And, even more surprisingly, sexy. An internal glittery sensation she hadn't felt in ages lit inside her, making her feel as effervescent as the champagne everyone was drinking.

'It is taken, but I suppose we could switch the name cards to make it yours. So long as you promise to be more entertaining than the real Oliver Bainbridge. He sounds a bit of a bore, don't you think?'

His eyebrows quirked at the challenge.

She pressed her lips forward in a *Go on, I'm waiting* moue. Was she flirting? *Crumbs.* She was flirting!

'Oliver's not exactly a name that soars up the sexy charts, is it? Would it help if I told you my middle name was Casanova?'

She hooted with laughter, and through a giggle managed to say, 'I think that would be worse.'

'Well, then...' He took her hand in his and raised it to his lips. 'Would you be satisfied if I were to stay plain old Oliver?'

He pressed the softest of kisses to the back of her hand, sending a spray of heat through her body, highlighting the more...*ahem*...erogenous zones.

This Oliver Bainbridge could be rather dangerous. Dangerous and yummy. The problem being, Princess Amelia Margit Sigrid Embla Trelleburg of Karolinska didn't find men 'yummy'. She found them *suitable*. Or *appropriate*. Or, in the case of her last boyfriend, *well-vetted*.

But Lia, for the very first time in her life, fancied a bit of *yummy*.

Her eyebrows arrowed up into what Jonas

called her 'imperious Empress' expression. 'I suppose the name will have to do until we come up with a better one. Now, then, as we're seated next to one another, do you think you'll be able to keep me entertained all night? I have very high standards, you know.'

Who *was* she—and where had plain old Lia gone?

'I shall endeavour to do my very best.' His lips twitched as if they'd just shared a private joke of a much more carnal nature. 'If you'll allow a humble paediatrician the pleasure of trying?'

'Oh, the pleasure is all mine,' she said grandly, knowing as she did so that never before had truer words been spoken.

CHAPTER TWO

So *THIS* WAS Princess Amelia of Karolinska—
AKA Dr Trelleburg.

She was far more beautiful than the handful
of staff photos he'd seen on his weekly visits
to The Island Clinic. And…dared he say it?…
she was funnier than he would've thought. If
this had been a blind date, he'd have wanted
another. And very likely another after that.

But it wasn't. It was a formal charity event.
And, whilst their banter was fun and light-
hearted, at times crackling with a few unexpected frissons, no doubt the haughty humour
would turn out to have an edge…an icier hue…

He pulled out her chair, which she accepted
with thanks and, if he wasn't mistaken, her
cheeks pinkened with a hint of shyness.

Oliver dialled back his cynicism. It wasn't
her fault she'd been born to a royal family and

defaulted to haughty as a form of humour. Just as it wasn't his fault that he was—

'Champagne?'

He waved it away out of habit.

'On call?'

Princess Amelia nodded at his card which—yes—did say what he did and where he did it. Standard practice for events like this, so that guests of honour didn't have to be embarrassed by getting the details of would-be donors incorrect.

He shook his head and answered mostly truthfully. 'You're not drinking, so I thought decorum dictated that I do the same.'

The last thing he wanted to be around a woman whose presence was tugging at the more primitive parts of his body was drunk.

She pushed her lips into a thoughtful pout, then said, 'Hmmm… I would've thought an Oliver Bainbridge, no matter where he stands on the sexy name scale, would have a bit more backbone than that. A man who sets his own agenda, not someone who would kowtow to the outdated dictates of another country's aristocracy.'

To mask the vein of truth she'd unearthed, he

grabbed his chest and feigned pulling a knife out. 'Oh, did you, now?'

Oliver laughed—more at himself than anything. She was right. He'd never expect anyone to treat him differently because of who he was. It was nice to see she didn't expect people to change their behaviour around her just because of her parentage. 'And here I was thinking I was just being polite. Tell me…' he met her clear-eyed gaze head-on '…what else do you think an Oliver Bainbridge would be like?'

She tipped her head to the side and gave him a scan that felt more physical than it should have.

She wouldn't know it, of course, but he'd grown up in a world remarkably similar to hers.

'I think he'd be kind,' she began, 'this Oliver Bainbridge character.'

He nodded. If kindness was a religion, he'd be kneeling at the altar.

She tapped her chin. 'Diligent in his line of work. It's a calling, not a job.'

He smiled at this. Yes. She'd got that right as well.

She smiled back, and another hit of connection flared between them.

'I think he likes reading stories to his patients when they're sad.'

He let out a low whistle. She was good. *Very* good.

'Sounds like a wish list,' he said, wondering if he could tap into her psyche the way she'd tapped into his.

'Hmmm...' she smiled, non-committal, as she took a sip of sparkling water.

'When do I get to turn the tables?' he asked. 'See what my inner crystal ball reveals about you?'

'You don't,' she quipped lightly.

His smile broadened. They really were similar. Happy to talk endlessly about work and other people, but when the observations turned personal...? Not so much.

'That's not exactly fair, is it?'

She gave an untroubled shrug, her shoulders shifting under the light blue fabric that somehow made her skin look like golden sugar.

He caught himself imagining what it would taste like if he were to drop kisses along it, then abruptly stopped the careless fantasy. A princess with a reputation like hers—private, private and even more private—would hardly be up for a bit of canoodling away from the crowd.

It was quite a feat to have kept herself to herself as much as she had on this small island. The Island Clinic was renowned for its ability to keep its clients' comings and goings out of the public eye as much as for its medical prowess, but she'd been here three years to his two, and they'd never once crossed paths. Granted, most of his time was spent at the St Victoria Hospital, rather than the clinic, but even so... There weren't that many places to grab a bite to eat.

Was she hiding something?

A twinge of the pot calling the kettle black bounced against his conscience. He met her gaze with a look he hoped said that he got it. He understood what a life weighted with expectations beyond your control was like. Suffocating. Lonely. Painful.

Something flared hot and bright between them as their eyes clicked and cinched.

Kindred spirit... That was the first thing he felt break through their magnetic connection.

Interested... That was the second.

Well, what do you know?

This evening was suddenly looking up in a very different and unexpected way. He'd anticipated a bit of dry chicken. Some uninspired speeches. The inevitable silent auction aimed at increasing donations beyond the breathtakingly high price of buying a table.

Not that raising money for a free medical clinic was a bad thing. Far from it. But an unexpected flirtation definitely improved the prospects of the evening.

He returned her appraising gaze, enjoying the way her hips shifted against the fabric of her dress as if he had actually run his fingertips along them.

She looked as if she could walk straight into one of those 'destination wedding' photo shoots that often populated the immaculate coves and beaches of St Victoria. Her skin was barely touched by make-up. A bit of mascara and little else. She had a golden tan that added a healthy glow to her pink cheeks. Her satiny white-blonde hair was all but begging him to run his fingers through it. And her light blue eyes were communicating exactly the same thing he was pretty sure his eyes were telling her.

I fancy you.

Oliver only just managed to restrain himself from leaning in to the soft cloud of scent she left in her wake as she turned away.

Three hours later he was properly captivated.

Lia wasn't a cardboard cut-out royal, as so many of them were at these events—shuttled in to make sure the money flowed, then shuttled back out through a private exit to a private car or a plane, back to their private residence.

She was cut from different cloth.

Funny. Beautiful. Charming. Passionate about her work and genuinely committed to the charitable work at The Island Clinic—which, if rumour was to be believed, had seen more film stars than some Hollywood studios had.

Yes, she was incredibly private, but she was as well-schooled as he was in the fine art of being born to shoulder the burden of your forebears and she knew how to hide it.

She'd managed to extract a bit of background from him. The fact that he'd been born and bred in the UK. A paediatrician by choice, not by family tradition. And the fact that, like her, he was very happy here on St Victoria, where if the sun wasn't shining the rain was falling, and all of it was beautiful, lush, tropical…and, like tonight, heated. Very heated.

He wanted her. More than he'd wanted a woman in a long time.

As if the heavens were assisting him the meal finished. After a whispered bit of news that the clinic's founder, Nate Edwards, wasn't able to kick things off, the dancing was set to begin. Oliver saw that the mayor, seated on Lia's left, was leaning across to ask for the first dance.

In a move he wouldn't have expected of himself, he decided to pip him to the post. Pushing his chair back, he held out his hand. Lia's eyes darted away and then back. Decorum dictated she should dance with the mayor, the more senior of the two in social profile, but as a doctor at St Victoria Hospital, which had a very close relationship with The Island Clinic, it wouldn't be too unseemly for her to dance with him instead.

As the conductor held the small orchestra in an expectant trill of flute and violin, he felt another flash of connection as she lightly put her palm on top of his. Moments later he was holding her in his arms. Her scent, the softness of her skin, the swish of her hair against his hand… He would be hard pressed to think of another moment in his life when he'd have been perfectly happy for the rest of the world to fade away.

His fingers lightly grazed her bare skin at the deep V in the back of her dress. She shivered.

'Cold?'

She shook her head, clearly unable—or un-willing—to put a name to what it was that had sent goosebumps skittering along her arms.

He knew what it was. Because he was feel-ing it, too.

Desire.

They didn't exchange another word for the duration of the song, but the space between them at the end was definitely much, much smaller than it had been when he'd first slipped his arm round her waist and pulled her to him for the slow, mesmeric dance.

When the music stopped she took a step back, her breath quicker than it should have been after a slow dance. He presumed she was going to excuse herself and accept a dance with the mayor, who was waiting rather expectantly at the side of the dance floor.

But she leant in close and, instead of saying

Thank you or *That was nice*, she whispered in lightly accented English, 'Do you want to go for a walk on the beach?'

He did. Very much so. But that didn't mean it could happen.

'Don't you need to stay?'

'Yes,' she answered, with a smile an outsider might have mistaken for meaning that she thought it was nice he was a children's doctor.

But everything about the electricity zinging between them was saying something else entirely. It was saying *I want you.*

A shared, unspoken understanding meant they knew they couldn't leave together. But that same understanding also made it clear that before the night was over they would be in one another's arms.

'Is an hour long enough?' he asked.

She nodded.

'Which beach?'

The one at the front of the hotel wouldn't do. Not with the crowds of tourists and locals flowing in and out of the bustling restaurants and hotel bars dotted along the main harbour.

His mind whirred with possibilities. 'Sugar Cove?'

She arched an eyebrow, then gave an infinitesimal nod.

For the crowds looking on, he gave a courtly bow of thanks. For Lia, he gave the inside of her palm a light press with his thumb. A touch he hoped indicated that he wouldn't let her down.

Then he walked away so she could meet some of the other guests.

After a tactical 'walking to be seen' stroll through the crowd, he paused in front of a large group of colleagues and pulled out his beeper. He gave his forehead a slightly dramatic run-in with the heel of his hand. He worked with kids. He was used to playing to a crowd.

'Ah, bad luck, Oli!' one of them called out, clearly rather jolly after the endlessly flowing champagne. 'Is that the hospital?'

He gave one of those *What can you do?* shrugs. 'Kids, eh?'

'We'll see you tomorrow, Ol!'

He gave them a wave and, because he believed in the cause, pulled out his chequebook and a pen. 'Better do this before I go...'

A chorus of 'Take cares!' and 'Hope everything's all right, Dr Bainbridge!' followed in his wake as he threw them a wave and then left the venue.

As he had an hour, he did actually swing by the hospital. His happy place.

He popped his head round the corner of a room that had a little girl in it he knew would far rather be anywhere else but in hospital. Yup. He was right. Élodie was wide awake and looking scared. His heart squeezed tight. He cared for all his patients, but there was something about Élodie that bored straight through to his heart.

'What are you doing up, love?'

The little girl looked across from her picture book and gave him a tearful smile. 'Dr Bainbridge!' Her smile faded. 'I'm *peeyops*!'

Oliver hid a smile. The creole word meant 'going crazy', and he could certainly relate. His fingertips were still tingling with the memory of holding Princess Amelia in his arms… alive with the anticipation of much more. *If*, he abruptly cautioned himself, that was why she wanted to meet.

Maybe he'd read it wrong. Perhaps she wanted to talk hospital logistics or… His stomach clenched at this thought. Or she knew who he really was.

Right. Distraction. That was why he was here. For both himself and Élodie. He scooped up a pile of fairy tales someone had donated a couple of weeks back and crossed to her.

'Why can't you sleep?'

She made a squishy face, then said, 'It hurts.' She tapped her chest and flopped back, her sprawl of dark, curly hair haloing around her on the pillow.

'Why don't you have some oxygen?'

Her face crumpled. 'I just want to be normal!'

His heart ached for her. Élodie's health demanded that she acknowledge that she wasn't. She'd contracted malaria a few years back, in the wake of a devastating hurricane, and as she already had weak lungs from her asthma, was prone to recurrences.

'When can I go home?' she asked.

Oof. That was a weighted question. The hurricane that had compromised her health had also taken her mother and father. She lived with her aunt and uncle now, but they had several teenaged children of their own and, with low-paying jobs, found Élodie's health problem a burden they struggled to fund and, more often than not, didn't attend to. He knew they used her hospital visits as a form of the day care they couldn't afford, but the alternative—leaving her on her own—simply wasn't an option.

Before he could answer, Élodie gave him a narrow-eyed gaze, then beamed. 'You look like a prince. Have you been to a ball?' Her small shoulders lifted and dropped as she gave a huge, painful-sounding sigh. 'Will I ever get to go to a ball?

Oliver's heart constricted. She'd been asking about leaving for a week now, but the hospital was the safest place for her. He hated that reality on her behalf. He hadn't been an orphan, but he knew what it was like to feel like an outsider in your home. As such, he'd privately funded a few extra days for her to stay in hospital, to ease the strain on her aunt and uncle and also, in all honesty, to ensure he could keep a closer eye on her.

He worried about her, and he knew he'd hold himself personally responsible if her health deteriorated outside of his watch.

'Soon, little one. You're doing amazingly

well, considering how high your temperature was when you came in.'

'I suppose...' She frowned her displeasure that the malaria had come back at all.

He fanned out the books. 'So... Which one will it be?'

Élodie's eyes widened, her distress temporarily forgotten, as she pointed at one of the books. 'Can we read about a princess?'

Oliver gave a silent groan. Of all the nights to read about a princess! Why hadn't he checked the books before offering her a choice?

'Absolutely.'

He pulled a chair up beside her bed, and before he opened the book did a quick scan of her stats and gave a surreptitious glance at her chart, to check the last time she'd been given her pain meds. Then, with a smile, he opened the book.

'Once upon a time...' he began.

By the time Élodie had gifted him some thank-you sweeties—sour apple, her favourite—and he'd looked in on a couple of the other children, he was buzzing with adrenaline. He hopped into his Jeep and set off away from

Williamtown, the story of *Sleeping Beauty* still swirling round his head.

The fictional Princess had proved fairly tricky to woo but, after hacking down a palace's worth of thorns, discovering an entire sleeping royal court, including the most beautiful slumbering princess in the world, it appeared all the Prince had needed to do to restore harmony was give the Princess one life-affirming kiss to wake her from her slumber so that joy reigned and they all lived happily ever after.

He snorted. If only real life were that easy. Not that he was after wedding bells or any-thing—the drama that would ensue once his family got so much as a whiff of an heir to the family title would be off the charts—so he'd take the life-affirming kiss for now.

He tried to wipe his mother's inevitable dis-approval of a late-night liaison from his mind, then laughed. He was meeting a princess for a moonlit walk by the sea. His mother would be the first one to approve.

The cove was only a five-minute drive away from the hospital. One he knew like the back of his hand, because his seaside home was just around the corner. Lia wouldn't have had a clue that it was his favourite place on the island, and yet like someone who knew him like the back of their own hand she'd chosen his 'go to' spot.

No matter what mood he was in after an inevitably long day at the hospital, or an even longer one at The Island Clinic, from the moment he first stepped out onto the beach it felt like he was in a different world. Secluded, and slightly tricky to get to unless you were a local, it was surrounded by tiny footpaths unlit by streetlights. They were the only way to get there.

When he arrived—tie off, shoes off, warm sand beneath his feet and the phosphorescence of the waves doubly bright with the addition of the night's nearly full moon—he thought it would be impossible to find anywhere more romantic.

He was just about to begin undoing the buttons on his dress shirt when a female voice said, 'I thought that might be my job.'

CHAPTER THREE

WHAT?

Lia was beginning to feel as if an entirely different woman had poured herself into her body when she'd put on her gown tonight. Maybe it was just the dress, but… She didn't say sultry things like that. Or give naughty little smiles after she'd said them. Then again, she was hardly one to invite a man she'd met at a charity ball to a remote beach cove for a midnight walk either, so…

Was this a magic dress?

She looked at Oliver—still in his tux, minus the tie, which was hanging loosely round his neck. There was the tiniest hint of a five o'clock shadow. *Mercy.* She barely contained the urge to lick her lips. He was positively scrumptious. A little rumpled, perhaps. But who wanted perfect when history dictated that perfect was unsustainable?

This man… *Mmm…*this man was something

else. A man who knew his own way. Someone who'd tapped into a part of her she hadn't even known existed. The sexy seductress who felt every bit as powerful and self-possessed as he seemed.

This wasn't at all her normal modus operandi. And what was more she liked it.

Only a few hours in his company and already she liked herself more with him than without him. Which was something she'd have to cap, because it was the same dangerous path to 'head over heels in love' her parents had followed and that hadn't exactly ended well.

And yet it was very tempting to throw caution to the wind.

Just for tonight.

Obviously.

Not only was Oliver intelligent, funny, and openly passionate about his work as a paediatrician, he was just about the most attractive man she'd ever laid eyes on. Or perhaps he was attractive *because* of those things. He might not be everyone's cup of tea—there was a little scar on his left eyebrow, a smattering of freckles that arced up and over his nose that hinted at the boy he'd once been, and when he smiled the crinkles around his eyes betrayed a slightly weather-beaten aesthetic—but Lia liked every single centimetre of him.

Like a woman possessed, she watched herself reach out and tease open the top button of his shirt.

He exhaled at its release.

She skidded her fingertip down his Adam's apple, along the short hollow between his collarbones to the next button.

The air between them crackled with invisible electricity.

'Your dress only has the one tie?' he asked, after she'd released another button.

She watched his eyes drop to the wraparound cloth belt that held her dress together. 'Looks like it.'

He reached out to touch it, but she took his hand in hers with a *No, you don't* click of her tongue. 'Good things come to those who wait.'

She moved his hand to her hip.

Who on earth *was* she tonight?

Someone strong. Someone who went for what she wanted and didn't wait for the palace to give her its stamp of approval.

She'd never felt more alive.

She saw him clock the big straw tote she always brought whenever she went to the beach.

'Towels,' she explained as she released another button then met his eyes. 'And whatnot.'

She'd been given a bottle of the vintage *grand cru* champagne by the staff at the hotel after the event. She'd thought of saving it until her cousin came out in a couple of months, for his annual leave, but here and now might be the perfect place to drink it. If they were going to be sitting and chatting, that was...

'Whatnot?' Oliver's mouth twitched into a smile.

Medieval convent schools in Karolinska had never made much of a point of being 'down with the kids', so her vocabulary sometimes erred on the side of very old-fashioned. Tonight she was going to let that be an asset.

'Yes.' She undid another button, then met his eyes. 'Whatnot.'

There were plastic cups, a container filled with an array of sweet tropical fruit, and an opulently inviting box of chocolates. But she didn't want any of that now. She wanted him.

Instead of saying as much, she tipped her

head towards the sea. 'We might fancy a mid-night swim.'

'I didn't bring my bathers,' he said.

He didn't sound sad about that at all.

'Nor did I,' she countered.

He nodded, then tipped his head to the side so that the moonlight caught the fine cut of his jawline. He looked, just at that moment, as if he'd been sculpted.

He moved again, and before she could catch her breath she was in his arms and he was kiss-ing her. Softly at first. Inquisitively. He tasted of salty air, the tiny bit of white wine he'd had at the ball and, interestingly, of sweeties. Sour apple, if she wasn't mistaken. But mostly he tasted of that indefinable essence that made him irresistible to her.

Eau de Oliver Bainbridge.

Whatever it was, it consumed her.

Their breath became one as they touched and tasted each other. The soft rasp of his stubble against her lips made her draw in a quick breath. His hands gently cupped her face as he held her away from him to see if she was all right, then brought her in close for an even deeper kiss. One she never wanted to emerge from.

When they finally broke apart, he dropped one of his hands to her throat, his thumb lazily tracing her collarbone as his other hand slid down the entire exposed length of her back until it made contact with her dress. Their bodies organically arced towards each other. There was no mistaking his arousal.

'Should we take that swim?' Oliver tipped his forehead to hers. 'Cool down a bit?'

She knew what he was asking. Did she want to make love to him now, or cool things down so they had a chance to decide properly if they were making the right decision.

She did want to make love to him. And the pulse between her legs was doing its best to vote for immediate satiation of its desire. But she also didn't want this magical night to end. She'd never been skinny dipping before, and the thought of that warm tropical sea surrounding her naked body and his naked body, the two of them kissing with all that deliciously warm water around them…

She took one of his hands and moved it to the flimsy bow tied at her side. 'I think we should take a swim and then perhaps engage in a little…whatnot. If you're willing?' she tacked on, suddenly aware he might be the one trying to back out.

Having an HRH in your name tended either to pull in the wrong kind of suitor—the kind who was desperate for some sort of link to royalty—or, as had been her last experience, repel them because of the floodlights her family occasionally shone on her life. Even in a place as remote as The Island Clinic.

Oliver ran his fingers along the soft fabric of her dress's bow and then, as if he'd made a decision, moved his hand to her arm.

Her heart twisted with a tight ache of longing. She wanted this man. And she'd been certain up until about two seconds ago that he wanted her as well.

But he was right to step away. There was no future in this kind of physical attraction. Her parents' marriage was proof of that.

Besides, she tried to tell herself as her body screamed its protest, she liked her life the way it was. And Oliver had made it very clear he liked living a life under the radar. Dating a princess—even one five thousand miles away from home—simply didn't allow for that.

Oliver ran his fingers down her side, eliciting

another rush of goosebumps, and then, sensing her change of mood, pulled back again. 'Are you looking for a commitment, or one night of whatnot?'

He didn't colour the question in any way and she admired its openness. They were adults, both in their thirties. They had professional lives they clearly loved. His question was telling her all she needed to know. Whatever happened between the pair of them—one night, a few dates, something more—was up to her. Not out of a lack of interest…being this close to him assured her he was *very* interested…it was more a matter of consent.

So. The ball was in her court.

She made her decision. 'One night to remember seems a perfect way to end the evening, doesn't it?'

His voice was rough when he answered. 'As long as you're sure.'

In one fluid move she tugged the bow of her dress loose, revelling in the sensation of its fabric slipping along her body and down to the sand as she ran towards the sea.

'I want a night of freedom!' She whooped. 'A night of whatnot.'

If he wanted to join her, she thought as she ran into the sea, that was up to him.

She dived into the water, astonished at how luxurious it felt. Warm, sensual, moving her body with the gentle rhythmic undulations of the sea... Though she'd hardly thought of swimsuits as cumbersome, swimming naked in a moonlit sea with Oliver watching was on another level. Her body was positively thrumming with desire.

When she came up for air a few metres along and looked back to the shore she didn't see him at all.

Her heart sank.

Ah, well. She'd given him a choice and he'd made the sensible decision. Never mind. At least she could tick skinny dipping off her—

She felt a tickling against her legs, and then a whoosh of movement as Oliver surfaced next to her and pulled her into his arms. His body, fully naked, pressed against hers. She could feel his arousal as he pulled her legs up and around his hips and began to kiss her as if his life depended on it.

She felt his touch everywhere. His fingers tangled in her hair. His hand pressing against the small of her back to draw her closer to him. Then both of his hands were sweeping along her thighs and her bum as if she were a goddess, sent this one moonlit night for the express purpose of being cherished.

Soon enough she was returning his touch, her hands unable to resist touching his hair, his athletic shoulders, his chest. She dipped her head to give his nipples soft, swift nips, then raised her head to give him a salty kiss.

The water supported much of her weight, and he lifted her up so that he could caress and gently swirl his tongue round the taut tips of her breasts. She barely contained a moan of desire. He walked the pair of them into deeper water, so that when he lowered her for another hungry kiss, her entire body felt as though it had been submerged in their shared desire.

She'd never experienced a more erotic moment in her life. The soft breeze played amongst the droplets on her shoulders as the warm water brought them even closer together than they already were. They swam and kissed and touched and explored. It was the most intimate Lia had ever been with someone, and yet she'd never felt more comfortable in her own skin than she did here and now, with this man she might likely never see again.

'Are you warm enough?' he asked, after another soul-quenching kiss.

With the heat they were sharing? Oh, definitely.

'Mmm…but…' This was the tricky part. She didn't want to have sex without the all-important protection. 'If things progress… I'm not prepared.'

'My cottage is a two-minute walk away.' His voice was a low rumble of desire. 'I've got some things that will make "whatnot" safer. Shall we grab those towels of yours?'

He didn't have to ask twice.

Wrapped in huge fluffy towels, they rounded the corner of the cove to another, smaller inlet. When Lia saw where Oliver lived, she laughed with sheer delight.

Though it was bathed only in moonlight, and the finer details weren't entirely clear, Oliver's home would have put a luxury Swiss Family Robinson treehouse to shame. What looked to be four or five rooms and open-walled seating areas dappled the treeline, hung like beautiful baubles above a small sky-blue wooden cottage with a gorgeous wraparound porch. It was, in short, a tropical tree house mansion.

She gave him a dry look—difficult to do when she was feeling exceedingly lusty and there were only a pair of towels between them. 'You call *this* a cottage?'

'It's got a picket fence, hasn't it?'

'Yes, but...' She dissolved into giggles. 'I still don't think this qualifies as a cottage.'

Oliver gave a self-effacing laugh. 'Well...it started that way.'

Lia shook her head in amazement. 'I can see why you chose paediatrics over geriatrics. You're a dreamer, aren't you?'

She thought of her own, largely undecorated living quarters that were part of the clinic's staff accommodation. The house itself was exactly the kind of thing people in Karolinska who wanted a luxury holiday in the Caribbean would daydream about during the long, snowy winters: a sky-blue cottage with a pristine white porch, dripping with flower baskets and other unexpected touches of luxury—an outdoor shower *and* bath, a 'widow's peak' balcony with a mosquito-netted daybed and, in her bedroom, a very, *very* large four-poster bed.

None of which she'd put her own mark on in the three years she'd lived there, as Oliver had with his own home. He was clearly a man who wanted to settle down, have a home. Whereas she... She was ever grateful for the tide that washed away her footprints, leaving not so much as a trace that she'd ever been there.

Oliver was grinning at her, obviously taking the backhanded compliment on the chin. 'I call it believing in possibility with a practical edge. I bought the cottage—all two rooms of it—when I moved to the island. It had been deserted after the hurricane and was barely habitable—which gave me an idea. Why not build up, rather than out? The tree canopy provides some protection from the winds, and... Well, who doesn't like a tree house?'

His enthusiasm was infectious. 'It really is amazing.' She held up her hands in awe. 'You've created a personalised paradise. Colour me impressed, Peter Pan.'

He grinned and gave a playful kick at the sand as if her praise had embarrassed him. When he looked up there was a very grown-up heat in his eyes that swept through her like wildfire.

'I guess that makes you my Tinker Bell.'

She gave an obliging laugh, only just catching a glimpse of something flashing across his face that unexpectedly tugged at her heart. It was sadness. Not a fresh grief. It was something that had become a part of him. She decided not to press. If his past was anything like hers, it was worth leaving precisely where it was.

'Well, if that means I can fly and get a magic wand I approve.'

He gave a self-conscious, *'Ha!'* and then explained as he led her towards the porch. 'It really did start out as just the cottage. Turns out I like to do a little DIY in my spare time.'

She shook her head, amazed. 'Your spare time sees a lot more action than my spare time.'

'I doubt that.' He ran the backs of his fingers along her cheek, then swept her wet hair into a loose knot at the nape of her neck as he dropped a kiss on her shoulder. 'You're a doctor. You know as well as I do that every day doesn't go as planned. We do what we need to do to regroup after work. I build things. I'm sure whatever you do is equally healing.'

The look he gave her was so honest, so complete in its belief that Lia's moral compass was as solidly grounded as his was, that a rush of emotion flooded her chest. There was absolutely no judgement in his tone. He believed in her.

She could fall for this man if she didn't watch herself.

'I sail,' she said, to fill the silence.

She'd grown up sailing, and whenever things had grown too lonely at boarding school, or too claustrophobic at the palace, she'd run down to the harbour, jumped onto her boat and relished the relief of feeling her mind slowly return to her body as she got further away from the shore.

Being alone was so much better than feeling lonely in the middle of a crowd. But these days she didn't sail so much to escape her life. It was more to give herself room to breathe between its more intense moments. Sailing a boat demanded her full attention—physical and mental—and, as such, was the best way to clear her mind after a long, difficult surgery.

She'd thought she had found the perfect balance. But this man... He'd built an actual dream house.

She tamped down the urge to ask him what

sort of dreams he'd had for inside the house when it was built, just as she could see him biting back an urge to ask her about her sailing.

They'd said one night only.

He took her hand in his and led her into the house, the atmosphere between them shifting once again.

With each step she felt the flickering desire she'd felt in the sea build and gain purchase. They barely made it to the porch before she had to kiss him again.

It was a porch that demanded moonlight kisses. It featured a wooden couple's swing and a well-loved hammock. There was a stack of books beside each of them. And there was, of course, a door that led up into the magical maze where, somewhere amongst the trees, was Oliver's bedroom.

When he swung open the door she felt another, indefinable click of connection. The small sitting room was immaculate. Not institutionally so—it looked comfortable—but there was something very familiar about it.

'Boarding school?' she asked, before she could stop herself.

He gave her a quick look of surprise and then released a self-effacing laugh. 'That obvious?'

'Takes one to know one. The only thing that's out of control in my place are the piles of books.'

He pulled her to him and gave her a light kiss on the lips. 'I have a feeling there's going to be something other than book piles that are out of control tonight.'

Heat rayed out from below her belly button. Oh, he had that part right.

With nothing but towels between them, Oliver was finding it difficult to control his more primal instincts. As he guided Lia up the stairwell his fingers twitched with the urge to tug the thick cotton away from that gorgeous body of hers and have her here and now. But if they were only going to have one night he wanted to make sure each moment was more memorable than the next. One-night stands weren't really his thing, but something told him tonight had to be the exception to his unspoken solid rule.

When they arrived on the next level she suddenly stopped, her blue eyes alive with pleasure.

'What?' he asked.

'I feel like I'm walking through your imagination.'

Her smile was both intimate and delighted as she wandered through his living room—a largely open-air space, which was much more homely than the room downstairs. Cushiony sofas. Tumbles of tropical plants. More books. And,—one of his favourite elements, on full, proud display here—the thick trunk of the tree the house was balanced in, soaring right through the middle of the room, complete with a swirl of solar-powered fairy lights.

She smiled at him, and the warmth of it hit him right in the chest.

'Your house is like those Russian dolls.'

'How so?'

'But instead of getting smaller and smaller, the rooms become more and more like the real Oliver.'

When he didn't answer she took a step back, as if questioning her own judgement and checking herself for having got it wrong.

He thought of telling her she was spot on, but he closed the space between them, responding with a light kiss on the cheek instead. If this really was going to be a one-night thing, keeping his emotional distance was probably wise.

The real answer, of course, was much more complex than a simple *yes*. To his parents the 'real' Oliver Bainbridge had a title. A family seat back in England. A reputation to uphold. And there were a few other, darker edges to his past he'd rather forget. As a result, the Oliver she was meeting was the Oliver he'd been for the last two years, here on St Vic. He had taken some getting used to, but at long last he really liked the guy. He was anonymous. Loved his work. The only thing that was missing was—

He checked himself. Best not go there. Tonight was about enjoying Lia's company.

When they climbed one more level and reached his bedroom she let out a happy sigh and clapped her hands. 'You sleep here?'

She twirled round in disbelief, then grabbed hold of his hands for balance when the spinning got the better of her. She looked young and beautiful and more at ease than he'd seen her all night.

'I'm insanely jealous! It's beautiful, Oliver.'

He drew her close, then turned her round so

he could wrap his arms round her waist and they could look at the room together. It was one of the highest rooms in the house, and his favourite.

At the centre was an enormous four-poster bed, featuring the towering tree trunk at the back. As was necessary in any tropical country, the bed was shrouded in diaphanous mosquito netting, billowing in the soft breeze. The hush-hush of the receding waves upon the beach were all the lullaby he'd ever needed here. But tonight wasn't about sleeping. Not yet anyway.

'Shower?' he murmured.

'Mmm...'

It was all the response he needed. He led her into the bathroom, which he'd managed to kit out with all the mod cons. Teak flooring stood in for tiles, and the water tanks hidden further up in the jungle canopy allowed for a nice hot shower out on the starlit balcony—or, on days that demanded a soak, for the filling of the claw-footed bathtub it had taken him and six other lads to pulley up the tree. The bath sat in pride of place at the open French windows.

He lit a couple of candles in the hurricane

lamps he'd hung about the place, watching their light flicker against the windowpanes and the solitary floor-length mirror. Then he turned her to face it, untucked the fold of towel that hid that beautiful body of hers, and kissed her neck with a low, 'Now, then. Where were we, exactly?'

Warm water was soon cascading over the pair of them as they caressed one another's soapy bodies. It was enough to push them both to the edge of insanity.

Lia had barely dried herself before Oliver scooped her up and carried her to the bed. He had no idea how, but as virtual strangers they seemed to share the same sexual heartbeat. Intense and fast shifted to slow and luxurious, then moved back to desperate for one another. Time became elemental. The tickling of an eyelash against his cheek made him feel as though an hour had passed. A kiss lasted for ever and not long enough. The pounding of her heart against his fingertips stopped time.

'Please,' she finally begged, her fingernails scraping the length of his back. 'I want you inside me.'

He swiftly sheathed himself and then lifted her, so that she was kneeling above him. Slowly, achingly slowly, she began to lower herself on to his erection. Hot, profound surges of desire made maintaining his control next to impossible. She teased him and dipped herself lower and lower, so that he felt, just for a nanosecond, what it was like to be completely surrounded by her.

'I want you...'

Her lips brushed against his ear as she lowered herself completely on to him, her fingertips moving along his sides until her light touch drove him to a near frenzy. In one swift move he slid his hands over the soft curves of her bum and flipped her on to her back. It was his turn to set the pace.

His hips latched with hers, pushing and thrusting into her honeyed essence, their movements organically syncing with the cadenced undulations of her hips. The energy connecting them grew in intensity until it became all-consuming...fiercely passionate in a way he never known himself to be. He wanted her, too. Their individual desires combined into one mutual longing. Something more powerful than he had ever felt.

No words needed to be exchanged for him to know that something bigger than either of them—the universe, maybe—had set everything that had ever happened in their lives into motion in order to bring them together on this one perfect night. It would, he had no doubt, set the standard for any relationship he would ever have in the future.

The warmth of the night and the heat of their bodies seemed to increase their energy, not drain it. As one, their bodies began to rock in a sultry, delicious rhythm, a beat that swiftly increased and then, without any sort of warning, hit a speed that seemed out of their control until finally, as one, they climaxed.

They made love a second time. More slowly… almost sleepily…but with a familiarity that hinted at a long-term relationship—which, for the second time that night, struck Oliver as strange. Having Lia in his arms gave him a warm, comfortable feeling of déjà-vu. But he'd definitely never met her before. There would have been no forgetting someone who tugged at his more primal elements with such precision. And yet being with her felt…familiar. She'd got close in a way none of his girlfriends had. As if they were two people unable to resist the magnetic lure of an attraction that went far deeper than the physical.

When dawn came, she looked at her watch and started saying something about the forty-minute drive to the clinic and a long day on the surgical ward. Her reminder that this had been a one-off.

He made her a cup of coffee and didn't press to see her again. They sat on his porch, watching the sea birds dip and dive as a glittering shoal of fish shimmered past, the silence between them light and comfortable. Not a hint of expectation weighted these last moments they would spend together. If they met again…he would welcome it. If they didn't…he now knew being with someone just the once could mean much more than he'd ever believed possible.

She handed him the coffee mug and gave his lips a soft peck, after which she thumbed off some lipstick. 'Sorry,' she said.

He caught her wrist and dropped a kiss on it.

'Don't be.' He took her other wrist in his hand and gave it a kiss as well. 'For balance.'

The smile they shared was complicit and warm—and more than that it was kind. A smile between two people who understood that they had shared something both beautiful and rare. A perfect night.

'Thank you,' she said, shouldering her tote, which still held the champagne and chocolates. They'd not needed any help in the aphrodisiac department.

'Thank *you.*'

He got up with her and watched until she disappeared round the far edge of the cove without so much as a farewell wave.

That's how it is with princesses, he thought with a rueful smile as he began to get ready to head into the hospital. *One minute you're dancing together at a ball, with nothing between you but a shared heartbeat and stardust, and the next...*

He looked out to the sand where—ha!—a gold flip-flop had fallen from her bag. It was no glass slipper, but he'd remember her by it.

Who was he kidding? He'd remember her

without it. From this moment on he'd always have a part of his heart bearing the imprint of Princess Amelia of Karolinska.

CHAPTER FOUR

One month later

'HE WAS LUCKY.' Lia lifted her hands away from the patient and, after peeling off her surgical gloves and popping them in the disposal bin, gave her lower back a much-needed knuckle-rub.

Thirty-two years old was a bit young to start feeling the aches and pains of standing at the surgical table, but…who knew? Her whole body was being weird lately. Stress, maybe. It had been crazy busy over the past month. So much so she'd only just managed to overcome the urge to drive to the other side of the island and accidentally-on-purpose run into a certain paediatrician at the St Victoria Hospital.

Realising her team were still looking at her, she held up a set of crossed fingers. 'Let's hope he gives up the motorcycle and finds a safer mode of transport.'

She wasn't one to be preachy, but on an island where 'open-air transport' was the preferred means of travel, she wished holidaymakers in particular would pay attention to the speed limit. It was there for a reason. St Victoria was a spider's web of curvy roads, and the more mountainous tracks, like the road the patient had been driving on, were made up of sharp-angled switchbacks.

He was lucky he'd crashed on the road, where their helicopter had been able to airlift him to the clinic, and not at the bottom of a cliff. As things stood, the blood clot she'd just removed from his brain had been milliseconds away from changing his life for ever. And not for the better.

A sudden wave of nausea swept through her.

Uh-oh. She'd thought she'd curbed her queasy stomach over the last couple of days with some healthy doses of chicken soup.

'Okay. We can close now.' She needed to get out of here. And fast.

'So he's clear? We can talk to the family?' asked Nate Edwards, her chief of staff.

Not an unfair question about such a high-profile patient, but she really had to get to the ladies' room.

'Lia?' He called after her, even though she was halfway to the door. 'What do I tell the family? Is he in the clear?'

She tried to sound bright as she fought yet another wave of nausea. 'You know how I feel about pronouncing someone in the clear.'

She headed for the door, simultaneously assigning closing procedures to her team and trying to visualise the fastest route to the closest private restroom.

Nate bounded ahead of her and held open the operating theatre door for her. 'I know. I know. "Saying a patient is in the clear puts them right back in the danger zone."'

'Close.' She gave him a playful elbow in the ribs as her dislike of being misquoted briefly overrode her queasiness. 'Saying a patient is in the clear makes them *behave* as if they haven't just had brain surgery—and *that* puts them right back in the danger zone.'

Nate tugged off his face mask so that she could see his smile. 'Thanks for jumping to the fore on this one,' he said.

'Pleasure.'

Late-night calls were something she'd been used to in her days of training with the military back in Karolinska. Back then a pre-dawn alarm had meant putting herself through brutal physical workouts or studying as if her life depended upon it—because out in the battlefields someone else's life eventually would.

Her family had put a sharp halt to her doing active duty, like her cousin, but she saw her work as a neurosurgeon as a similar call to service. She'd never leave a patient in the lurch. Especially one in critical care.

Her smile turned serious. 'Ryan was lucky he had the accident on St Vic and not on any of the other islands.'

Nate shook his head and gave a soft laugh. 'Spoken like a true neurosurgeon.' His expression sobered. 'His wife's probably thinking he would've been luckier if he hadn't had it at all.'

The comment landed with an unexpected barb. Up until now, Lia had never given a second thought to anyone worrying about *her* if she had an accident.

Her hands swept over her belly. 'I've got to dash. Sorry, Nate.'

Her boss gave her arm a quick squeeze, then

excused himself. She knew he would give Ryan Van Der Hoff's family the good news. Lia preferred to stay out of that sort of thing—particularly when there was a celebrity involved. And Ryan had starred in an international spy series that just about everyone in the world seemed to have watched.

As far as medical centres went, this one was at the top of the list in maintaining privacy and offering service with a gilt edge. Not actual gold, of course, but the service here was off the charts. Nate was a great boss as well. As someone who hated the limelight as much as their patients did when it came to personal matters, Lia was always happy to leave the *Good news, the surgery went well* talks to Nate.

You never knew if the paparazzi had managed to weasel their way in, or if a patient's nanny had been paid to surreptitiously take snaps of the medical team that had just performed life-saving surgery on her employer. It was rare. But it happened.

All she wanted to do was her job. Something she couldn't do when she was fighting this extreme—suddenly the penny dropped—*nausea*!

Twenty minutes later, with a test stick in her

hand, Lia could barely hear for the buzzing in her ears. Pregnant? There was only one man who could be the father, but... *Pregnant*?

Equal measures of hope, fear, panic and, most surprising of all, undiluted joy bounced around her chest as she tried to still her thoughts and wrap her brain around this new reality.

She was pregnant with Oliver Bainbridge's child.

Energy charged through her, almost physically escorting her out to her car so she could drive over to his side of the island, climb up that wild treehouse of his and into his bed, and pop the news. Open it up to fizz and delight like the champagne they'd never ended up drinking.

Then that energy crackled and crashed through her heart, surging up to her brain.

What was she thinking? No. She shouldn't tell him. She shouldn't tell anyone. Not until she'd figured out a bulletproof plan to keep the palace's controlling tendrils off her baby.

The palace.

An icy shudder swept down her spine.

She glanced at her watch.

The staff at her grandmother's office would just be getting into the office about now.

The temptation to bang her head repeatedly against a wall seized her.

She should have put together this puzzle on her own—without the aid of a pregnancy test. Her period was late. Her breasts were…well, rather buxom these days. Her lower back hurt when it never had before. And, of course, the nausea.

It was just…

A child.

She was going to have a child.

Someone she could love without rules and regulations—

Her hammering heart pulled up short, then froze in place.

Princesses from Karolinska didn't have children out of wedlock. They had very public weddings and magazine-friendly honeymoons, and did photo shoots a minimum of a year later with their grinning husbands by their side as they celebrated the birth of their children, had a few days off, then gave their lives over to supporting The Crown and snipping red ribbons at charity events—

Her heart launched back into action.

Husbands. She didn't have a husband. Oliver

had been more than happy to have their night together be a one-off, so it was more than likely he wouldn't want to be a husband—let alone be *her* husband.

She could try asking him…

Her heart lodged in her throat, making even a practice run impossible.

Marrying a man she'd met a sum total of once was right up there in the Very Bad Ideas department. It might even be the actual worst idea ever.

Her parents had met and married in a matter of weeks, and look how well that had turned out. One wandered round the palace like a robot, dutifully carrying out his royal duties as assigned to him by his parents, the King and Queen. The other, a commoner had fallen so very much in love with a prince, and given him a baby daughter, but had been held in contempt by The Establishment, ultimately leading not only to her divorce, but to her walking away from her daughter as if she was too cruel a reminder of that chapter of her life.

So, no. Marrying the stranger paediatrician who had made her tummy do funny things was not a good idea.

Her heart, already battered from wrapping itself round the revelation, squeezed so tight she could hardly breathe.

The palace would want to take over her life the instant they knew. Their meddling had been at the heart of her parents' break-up and she didn't even have a relationship to break up. How would they deal with that? Give her one? Pre-vetted?

Too easily she pictured a dungeon down in the bowels of her grandparents' castle...dark, dingy, and filled to the brim with prospective husbands for wayward princesses.

Her heart slipped down her throat, then free fell to just above her baby, a sharp breath only catching it short of landing right on it.

Interesting...

She really wanted to protect it.

She pictured Oliver down in that imaginary dungeon, those lovely hands that had spent the night caressing and pleasuring her now strained as they wrapped around the thick iron bars, his beautiful, male, lightly stubbled cheeks pressed between them, calling her name again and again.

She scrunched her nose.

Pure poppycock.

She barely knew Oliver... Well... She knew that light kisses along his neckline tickled him. She knew that lowering herself onto him with the patience of a devotee made him groan with pleasure. She knew he smiled when he slept, that he smelt like the beach and pineapple and something else intangibly male.

Up until she'd met him, it had seemed as though she'd only ever had sex with past boyfriends. With Oliver, it had felt like making love.

Up until now, she'd thought of their night together as something precious. Unique. A rare moment held in a beautiful chrysalis of unspoken connection.

Because, her pragmatic side reminded her, they'd had absolutely no commitment to one another. A beautiful night of the best sex she'd ever had and then, before the sun had had a chance to rise, she'd been blowing him a farewell kiss from the doorway. *Sayonara,* sunshine.

Abruptly, painfully, as if an actual dagger was plunging into her heart, she felt the anguish of that day her mother had been escorted from the palace grounds lance through her.

That was what really happened when you married a royal.

Destruction.

She forced her breathing to steady. Giving herself a panic attack and passing out in a locked women's bathroom no one knew she was in wasn't going to help anything.

She splashed some cold water on her face, dragged a scratchy paper towel over the droplets, then stared herself in the eye.

This would be fine. All of it would be fine.

She dropped her gaze to her stomach and silently vowed to the teensy-tiny baby only just beginning its life in her belly that it would be fine, too. She'd do everything in her power to offer it the kind of childhood she'd never had. Be a mother who didn't bow to the power of their forebears.

Sure, people loved the tradition of the Karolinskan royal family, but it wasn't as if it was a religion. Or law. They were figureheads. Little more than the icing on top of a very decorative democratic cake. They needed to look to the future, not bow to the restrictive measures of the past.

Yes. She would look to a future in which her son or daughter would know the one thing she'd never had: freedom.

Okay. Good.

She gave her reflection a solid nod, as if she'd just come up with the perfect way to perform a difficult surgery. So that was settled. All she had to do was call the palace, tell them she was pregnant, then ring Oliver and let him know he was going to be a father but that he definitely didn't have to worry about marrying her because she had it all in hand.

She picked up her phone and thumbed through her contacts until she found her father's number. Protocol dictated that the palace be informed before the father of her child. Hopefully her father would help buffer the much stronger reaction she knew King Frederik and Queen Margaretha would have.

She forced herself to press the little green button on her phone. After two rings her father picked up.

'Lia? What's wrong?'

She winced. Trust her father to think she'd

only ring if she had bad news. A darker, more painful thought entered her heart. Perhaps hearing from her only made him think of all the bad things in his life. She, after all, was one of the main reasons his marriage had fallen apart.

'Papa.' The word felt as foreign upon her tongue as the two that were to follow. 'I'm pregnant.'

Two hours of explaining later, the call that now included her grandparents had reached a crossroads.

They wanted her to marry Oliver.

She did not.

'I don't think it's a good idea,' she persisted, not really wanting to go into detail about how little she knew him.

'We do,' her grandmother said, as if that put an end to the matter.

Lia rolled her eyes, thankful that this wasn't a video call. She'd offered them a thousand options apart from the one they wanted: love, marriage, baby carriage. There was one card left to play. She hadn't wanted things to go this far, but she didn't need their money, their status or, more to the point, their boa-constrictor-like rules.

'What if I give up my title?'

There was a deafening silence on the end of the line, followed by a very curt, 'I don't think going in that direction would be wise, Amelia.'

Grandmama. She always helmed the ship in moments like these.

Unfortunately for Lia, her grandmother had a point. The fall-out of such a move would be brutal. The one thing she'd ached for her entire life was to feel as if she was part of a big, happy family. She'd got the 'big' part. Just not the 'happy'.

And walking away would mean the tenuous threads of connection she had to her father would be severed for ever. Her grandparents would pretend she'd never existed. Her beloved cousin Jonas would be told communicating with her was forbidden. Finding her mother at this juncture would be a) impossible and b) really stupid, because all she'd be proving was that history really did repeat itself.

She broke the silence. 'I'll talk to Oliver.'

'Perhaps you should leave that to us,' her grandfather cut in.

'No.' She shook her head at the phone and involuntarily ground the word out a second time. 'No. This is my...*situation*. I'll talk to him.'

'And tell him what, exactly?' her grandmother asked, as if she'd just smelt something vile and was demanding to know its source.

'The truth,' Lia snapped back, fatigue fraying what little remained of her patience.

'Which is...?' her father asked. 'What is the truth?'

Lia stopped short. She'd been about to say that she was going to tell Oliver the palace was demanding they get married, and that if he was prepared for a life of being micro-managed he could go for it, but she wasn't all that keen, so if he was all right with it she'd be looking to move to another island. Alone. Maybe not this nanosecond, because she really liked her job and would definitely need an income as the palace would for sure be cutting off her allowance. And, no, she didn't want child support. She didn't know what, if anything, she wanted from him...

All of which reminded her that this was her father, asking her how she was going to treat the father of her child.

It was the first genuine curiosity she'd heard

from him in years, and unexpectedly it softened the shard of unspent anger she'd held on to at the fact he'd sent her away to boarding school so young.

'I'm going to tell him I'm pregnant and that I want to keep the baby.'

'That's it?' her grandmother asked, in a tone that made it distinctly clear she was turning puce with anger right now.

'That's it.'

'And then what?'

'I'll listen to what he has to say, and we'll take it from there.'

Lia looked at her phone and ended the call. She turned it off, just to ensure it wouldn't ring again in five seconds, with her irate grandmother the Queen demanding she show more respect to The Crown.

This was about her, Oliver and their baby, and no one else. They would decide what they wanted to do and then they would tell the palace.

CHAPTER FIVE

'SHALL WE SHAKE on it?' Oliver knelt down so that he was at eye-level with the five-year-old who had quite an impressive bump on his forehead.

'But I like going on the slide with my friend,' came the plaintive reply.

Oliver laughed. 'I know. Going on the slide with a friend is fun. But what if their head accidentally hits yours when you've already got a bump? Probably best to slide solo for the next couple of weeks.'

The little boy shot a *Do I have to?* look at his mum, whose *Yes, you do* expression left little room for interpretation. He stuck out his hand and reluctantly shook Oliver's.

For a millisecond Oliver let himself wonder what it would feel like to hold his own child's hand in his.

If things had been different…

If things had been different he probably wouldn't be here, treating this lovely little chap.

He held his grip on the small hand in his, honouring the trust that came with the gesture, then let go, gave the lad a smile and closed the moment with a high five.

Wondering about things that hadn't come to pass or, more to the point, might never happen wasn't worth the airtime.

He opened the door for the pair of them, reminding the boy's mother to bring him in if he began to be sleepy at unusual times or exhibited any of the other signs of concussion outlined on the cheat sheet he'd written out for her.

A glimpse of white-blonde hair caught his eye mid-sentence. His chest filled with a huge, hopeful inhalation, then froze in place when it disappeared. It couldn't have been Lia. Not in this wing of the hospital anyway. Unless... Would she be looking for him?

She'd not broken the 'one night only' decision they'd made, and he'd respected that. It hadn't stopped him hoping their paths might cross again, though. What they'd shared— the electricity—hadn't just been physical. It had run deeper. Their connection had been...

visceral. As if they already knew one another. Two halves suddenly, finally, becoming whole. Which, of course, was insane. They were strangers. Strangers who had shared one extraordinary night.

'Dr Bainbridge?' the mum said, loudly enough to suggest she'd already said it once before.

'Yes…sorry?' He forced himself to refocus.

'Should he not stay the night?'

'No, honestly,' Oliver assured her warmly. 'I know a bump of that size can seem frightening—and, be warned, it will go some unusual colours—but he passed all the cognisance tests and seems right enough in himself. I think he's walked away with a bruised ego, more than anything.'

The mum laughed and said, 'Boys. You can't stop them from pushing things to the limit, can you?'

Oliver laughed along, feeling the sliver of his heart that ached for children of his own taking up a fraction more room in his chest than it normally did. Was it meeting Lia that had made his hunger for a child, a family of his own, inch to the fore over these past few weeks?

No, he thought, struggling to keep the anger

at bay. It was having the option taken from him before he knew it even was an option.

He shook his head, to clear it of thoughts of the defining moment that had played a role in bringing him here to St Victoria. Though it had been nearly six years ago now, it had left wounds that should've been healed by now— perhaps by a family of his own— but had somehow always festered. Staying single, focusing on his work—those things had kept the raw pain of his past at bay. But nothing yet had allowed him fully to heal.

He looked down at the little boy who was beaming up at him.

Moments like this helped.

He thanked them, then waved off the mum and her son, his last patients of the day, and went back into his office to finish up his paperwork.

'Oliver?'

He turned, so startled by the sight of the woman standing in his doorway that words logjammed in his throat until he finally managed to croak, 'Your Highness—'

'Lia,' she corrected him tightly. 'Can we talk? One of your colleagues...' she pointed vaguely down the corridor '…said you were finished for the day.' Her brows drew together. 'Maybe somewhere outside the hospital?'

For a nanosecond he thought she was going to suggest another swim, but she looked serious. Too serious.

'Of course. Is this—? This isn't about a patient, is it? A professional consult?'

She gave her head a solitary shake in the negative. 'It's personal.'

The way she bit out the word dropped a lead weight in his gut. This didn't sound good. Had someone taken pictures of them swimming in the moonlight? It was exactly the sort of photo that could win a paparazzo a healthy pay cheque. Unless, of course, they were trying to blackmail her with it.

This was just one of the reasons why he'd come here. To escape the prying eyes of the press. So far he'd been lucky. He'd never courted the society papers back in the day. Had only ever appeared in the Easter and Christmas photos his mother always insisted upon, trying to keep up with royalty. As if! They were in another league of aristocracy. One his parents kowtowed to every waking moment of their lives. More because it was ingrained in them than anything, but still…

His anonymity here was a freedom Lia had never known. He felt for her. From what he'd seen, she only ever used her title for good, and if it was now being turned against her… Well… The world was a crueller place than he'd given it credit for.

Stemming a few colourful words, he grabbed a light parka off the back of his chair, pulled his office door shut behind him and locked it. 'I know a place.'

Her features softened in gratitude. He fought the urge to pull her into his arms and comfort her. She seemed so vulnerable, so frightened… his heart ached for her. But if this *was* blackmail, or pictures destined for a gossip magazine, the last thing he wanted to do was add fuel to the flames.

St Victoria Hospital was open to all—unlike the exclusive clinic where she worked—so the fact that she'd ventured out to find him, where paparazzi might easily be lurking, meant that whatever this was, it was screaming *Important!*

With her silent agreement, he led her to the discreet exit towards the rear of the hospital where he was parked. He drove them to one of the higher outcrops overlooking William-town, that featured sprawling tropical gardens dappled with secret little nooks and crannies where, with any luck, they could have a private conversation.

Silently they walked along the paths, tension crackling between them, until Oliver pointed towards an area with a small brook running through it. He gestured to a bench, waiting for her to sit before he took his own seat.

'Your Highness—' he began.

'No.' She shook her head. 'Please. It's Amelia…or Lia. Or—' her voice shook slightly as she swallowed, then forced herself to continue '—or the mother of your child.'

The news hit him like a wrecking ball. Bashed into his heart and then lodged there, where, in the blink of an eye, it turned into a hot, brilliant ball of sunshine.

'Seriously?' He shook his head in disbelief. They'd used protection. Was this real? A chance to be a father? 'You're…you're pregnant?'

She nodded.

'You're going to keep it?' he asked, before he could stop himself.

She looked at him as if he were mad even to consider otherwise. He forced himself to re-group. This was Lia, not Sarah. Lia had chosen to tell him about the pregnancy, to include him. Surely she wanted this baby?

'So…if you're going to keep the baby, if it's what you want, why do you look so serious? So…' He sought a gentler word and couldn't find one. 'Unhappy?'

Lia dropped her head so he couldn't see her eyes, and mumbled something he couldn't quite make out.

He put his hand on her shoulder, then crooked his finger under her chin so they were looking at one another properly. Her light blue eyes glistened with tears.

'They want us to be married,' she bit out, as if the idea were detestable.

'Who?' He shook his head, confused.

'The palace,' she explained, just as he came to the same realisation. 'My grandparents and I spoke early this morning and they have spoken to the council—' She stopped herself, as if the life had been drained out of her, then met his gaze and said, 'The King and Queen of Karolinska will not have any heir to the throne born out of wedlock.'

'Fine.'

Lia's clear blue eyes blazed as if he'd just insulted her. 'What?'

'Fine. Good. Yes. I'll do it.'

Oliver clapped his hands together and gave them a rub, trying to channel the adrenaline coursing through him and failing. Whatever it took. He'd do it. There was no chance he was stepping away from another chance to raise a child. His child. Their child.

'Sooner the better.'

'You don't want to think about it?' she asked with a dry laugh.

'No.'

There was a side of him that was telling him to slow down. Think about it. But he wanted to lift her up and twirl her round. Shout, *I'm going to be a father!* so loud the entire island heard. He wanted to take care of her. Peel her grapes. Swaddle her in cotton. Rub her feet. Whatever it took.

But he could see she was anxious, weighing up the options—and why wouldn't she? Her life and her body were changing for ever, and it was all so unexpected. Understandable, then, that she might not seem excited. Even though for him—whether he wanted it to or not—an ancient, protective, paternal instinct was overriding everything else.

Lia's features were decidedly wary. 'You know what marrying me means, don't you?'

He shrugged and looked around, as if the answer was obvious. 'Live our lives, raise our child—' He stopped himself as the penny dropped. 'The palace will want full coverage of the new royal baby.'

Lia nodded. '*And* the engagement *and* the wedding. If there is one,' she added gravely, her expression now completely guarded. 'It's not all glitz and glamour, you know.'

He nodded. He knew. First-hand, he knew.

'We won't be going to galas like the one where we met every night. I won't be prancing around in a tiara.'

'That's a shame,' he said, realising too late that she was in no mood to make light of the matter. And she was right. A child's future was at stake, and her life was about to change. Both their lives were about to change.

She gave a heavy sigh and dropped her head

into her hands. 'They haven't had the council vote yet, so there's still a chance they won't make me do it.'

'Make *us* do it,' he corrected firmly. Whether or not she liked it, they were in this together.

She sat up straight, her expression morphing from helpless to defiant. 'We can't...we can't just let them play us.'

'It's not playing if we set the rules.'

'We don't have the power to set our own rules. Not with them.' Her laugh was utterly bereft of humour. 'Besides... You don't know me. You're not in love with me. You won't fight to the death for me.'

She held her hands apart and stared at him as if the last condition was the most crucial.

'I'd do *anything* for you—and for our child.'

There must have been something in his voice that reached her heart, because her next question sounded softer, as if he just might have cracked open the doors of possibility.

'Why?'

Everything in him stilled. This was a moment that could change the rest of his life. It was up to him if it was for the better or, more worryingly, for the worse.

He took her hands in his and looked her straight in the eye. 'I want to be a *parent.*'

The word seemed to resonate. She nodded, sucked in her teeth, wrinkling her brow as she considered him. 'Let me guess… Boarding school as early as they would take you?'

He smiled at how easily she'd made the connection. 'Yup.'

'Snap.'

Their smiles broadened and held long enough for them to exchange a mix of relief and empathy at this shared understanding, but his was swiftly tinged with guilt.

He should tell her the story. The whole story.

He curled his hands into fists, trying and failing to tamp down the vein of pain he'd thought long since extinguished.

Lia wanted to keep the baby, but it was her body. Her life. He respected that. Yet he couldn't forget the fact that his ex-girlfriend had taken matters into her own hands when she'd found out she was pregnant.

They'd been finishing their internships at a hospital in Oxford, filling out application after application for the futures neither of them had been able to wait to begin, when, one day she had casually informed him that she'd fallen pregnant but had 'sorted it'.

He had understood that it was her body, and her choice to make—that she was on the verge of a new life that didn't include a baby and so was he. Yet he would have been happy to support her, make a life with her and their baby. It had hurt that she hadn't wanted to discuss it with him, or considered his feelings in any way just as his parents had done on countless occasions.

'You'll stay with Nanny.'

'You leave for boarding school on Monday.'

'You'll be home in time for six as your father needs you for a father-son photograph for the papers.'

It was why living here was about as close to heaven as it got. *His* life. *His* decisions. *His* future.

But now he was going to be a father.

'What kind of parent do you want to be?'

Lia's question was so quiet it was almost as if she had thought it rather than spoken it.

'A *present* one,' he answered, with enough darkness to make her raise her eyebrows.

She stared at him hard, then looked away—as

if his answer had raised a thousand new questions, none of which she knew how to ask.

His had been a soulless upbringing, by parents whose only real interest in having a child had been producing an heir. Job done, they'd left his upbringing to staff—which, to be honest, had been perfectly fine. Perhaps wise beyond his years, he'd never been compelled to seek love where he knew it couldn't and, more to the point, *wouldn't* be returned. Which was why, when his relationship had gone south and his medical internship had been completed, he'd come here to St Victoria—to live an anonymous life as plain old Dr Oliver Bainbridge.

Lia shifted on the bench, then swept her hands across her belly. The reality that their child was growing in there hit him afresh.

He was going to be a father.

A husband, if—

Well, there were a lot of ifs.

If Lia would have him.

If the Karolinskan Crown was satisfied by him.

If he thought he'd be doing the best by his child by marrying her at all.

Because once she found out he came with his

own set of aristocratic baggage that symbiotic link he thought they shared might evaporate as quickly as the morning cloudbursts here did.

Some women—like his ex—simply weren't suited to marrying into a family like his. He closed his eyes at the memory of his parents meeting Sarah. Her lack of a title hadn't made for warm chitchat over the canapés. But, to be fair to his parents, Sarah hadn't exactly been all smiles and how-do-you-dos either. She'd talked about how outdated the aristocracy was, and how large estates like the one he'd grown up on and would one day inherit were shameful symbols of a past mired in inequality and the unfair bias of bloodlines rather than merit.

She'd been rude.

They'd been rude back.

None of it had ended well.

He blamed himself. He should have realised earlier that it would never work.

Moving here had seemed the best way to try and chisel away at a 'to-do' list that had seemed impossible back in England. He really did want to meet a girl and fall in love…have a family of his own. The trouble was, shaking off the darker edges of his past wasn't easily done. It wasn't how he was built, to turn his back on everything.

He'd thought of relinquishing his title, but the anguish he knew it would cause his parents wasn't the sort of pain he wanted to inflict on them. He didn't want to inflict *any* pain on them. He just… He wanted them to understand he was cut from a different cloth. A new cloth. One that didn't need to be edged in gilt or embroidered with his initials.

They weren't bad people—they were just of another generation in a so-called 'class above'. One that dotted its 'i's and crossed its 't's and had five-thousand-acre estates and stately homes that echoed with emptiness when they should be filled to the brim with life, laughter… grandchildren.

He pulled a couple of bottles of water out of the backpack he'd brought from his car—keeping some there was a habit he'd developed when he'd first moved to the hot, tropical island. He offered Lia one and then, after taking a swig of his own, felt an idea hit. The fact he was heir to a dukedom would probably help his stance in whatever the Karolinskan palace thought of him, but it probably wouldn't help with Lia. He had a limited amount of time before she found out who he was, and something told him there was no chance she would agree to marry him until she got to know him.

The *real* him.

He took another swig of water, then said, 'Before you call the palace...how about you and I go out on a date?'

She crinkled her nose and half smiled at him. 'What?'

'You know...' His own grin grew as he continued. 'One of those old-fashioned things. Dinner and a movie?'

She snorted. 'You want to go to the movies?'

He shrugged. 'Your call. Movies. Dinner. A walk on the beach.'

Now she outright laughed. 'Walking on the beach is what got us into this pickle!'

Flashes of their shared night returned to each of them. Their eyes met and the air between them crackled with electricity—a physical reminder of the sexual chemistry they shared.

'Good point.' He got down on one knee, then looked her in the eye, enjoying the return of that crackle of attraction. 'Lia?'

'Yes?' she replied, still wary, but also struggling to keep a smile off her face.

'Would you like to join me for dinner tonight?'

She burst into hysterics. 'Oh, thank God. I thought you were going to push the marriage thing. I seriously would have to consider moving to a desert island if you were that quick to agree.'

He let the comment lie where it had landed. Between them. He wanted to get married. She didn't. But she'd pushed the door of possibility open just a little bit further.

Just enough space for him to stick his foot in it.

He rose and held out his hand. 'Have you ever been to Anton's Fish Shack?'

CHAPTER SIX

'IS THIS QUESTION eighteen or nineteen?'

Lia shrugged. She was losing count. 'Eighteen?'

Eighteen questions out of twenty and she still hadn't asked the important ones.

Namely, the *Do you really want to marry me?* question. There might be Crown Jewels and ermine capes involved, but there was also the proverbial shotgun.

How could someone marrying a woman under duress ever fall in love with her?

She parted her lips, felt the words surge up her throat and lodge there. She finally managed to squeak, 'Favourite colour?'

'Green.'

'Favourite fish?' Lia gave a pointed nod at the mouthful of fish Oliver was about to bite.

'The one in the film.' Oliver grinned.

'What? *Jaws?*' Lia joked.

'The stripy one that talks and makes jokes.' Oliver shook his head as if it were obvious.

Then he handed her a chip. An extra crispy one. Her favourite.

Lia couldn't help it. She sighed a little. 'You really were destined to be a paediatrician, weren't you?'

He grinned and looked down at the ketchup on his tray, which he'd squirted in two circles and one arced stripe. In other words, a smiley face. He dunked a chip along the length of the smile, then gave her a cheeky grin. Her heart skipped a beat as she saw a dimple appear. She fought the urge to reach out and touch it with her fingertip.

His smile changed as their eyes met. Softened. Then he licked his lips.

Her heart slammed against her ribcage and her vision blurred everything around her apart from his mouth. Too easily she could imagine climbing over the table and demanding a thousand kisses. Something she never, ever in her life considered doing. Her tongue swept along her own lips. His was a mouth she could easily enjoy kissing for the rest of her life.

Was that enough?

Could lust keep a couple together?

A car horn sounded, jarring her back into reality. This wasn't about lust. It was about love, and whether or not it was something they might ever have. Even more importantly, it was about mutual respect.

She considered the last hour they'd spent down here on the harbour. She pretty much hadn't stopped talking. He drew information out of her like water out of a tap. Not deep, dark feelings, more the tiny little things that made up the woman she was. Loving sapphire-blue— the colour of his eyes—mac and cheese being her favourite comfort food, especially if it was combined with her favourite activity: curling up with a good book on a rainy day.

She'd talked a bit about boarding school, leaving out the part about how achingly lonely she'd found it, and how rejected she'd felt by her father, who'd kept himself holed up in the palace, and her mother, heartbroken after her failed marriage, who had not only left the country, but the hemisphere, and was now pouring herself into a life of charity work on a remote island in Southeast Asia, proactively blocking out the fact she'd ever had a daughter.

She'd admitted to wanting a dog one day, to dreams of starting a vegetable patch because she loved baby carrots. And she'd confessed, with a flush creeping along her cheeks, how much she would love, love, *love* the impossible chance to relive some of her childhood, so that she could experience, 'You know…a childhood.'

Oliver nodded now, as if he'd been taking down the symptoms of an illness, then said, 'You know what they used to call me at school?'

Lia hazarded a guess. 'Doc?'

'Mr Fix-It.'

Lia tried and failed to shove sexy images of the adult Oliver with nothing but a tool belt around his waist, addressing her life's problems. 'Did you have a fix-it kit?'

He shook his head. 'First-aid kit.'

'Seriously?' Wow. Medicine really was his calling.

'It was mostly filled with sweeties and plasters, but…' something dark shadowed his eyes. 'I don't like seeing people in pain. Especially children.'

She felt a depth of compassion in his voice, as if he'd pulled her into his arms and assured her he would do everything in his power never to let her feel pain ever again.

Her phone rang. They both looked at the screen.

Grandmama.

Also known as the Queen.

'Want me to give you some space?'

She picked up the phone but kept her eyes on him and shook her head. If Oliver and she actually agreed to this insane wedding, he'd need to see the vice-like grip the palace could put on a person if it wanted to. It had ended her own parents' marriage. It could easily prevent hers from ever happening.

She put the phone on speaker. 'Hello, Grandmama.'

'Amelia? We've got some notes for you to take down,' her grandmother said, in lieu of something normal, like *hello.*

She rolled her eyes. No need to ask who 'we' was, but for Oliver's sake she did it anyway.

Queen Margaretha rattled off the names of her own press officer, the King's, her father's, and the palace's private secretary.

Her father was on the call, too, but noticeably silent. Tears pricked at the back of Lia's eyes as she wondered what it would've been like if she'd grown up with a father who had actually wanted her around. Who, when she'd been hurting, would have defended her.

She glanced across at Oliver and easily imagined him with a little first-aid kit by his side. One filled with sweeties and plasters. Maybe he still had it. He had, after all, smelt of candy that one magic night that had changed everything.

'Ready?' she whispered, bracing herself for a command to fly home or, just as terrifying, prepare for the Princess Faux Pas Posse to arrive.

'What's that noise? Are we on speaker? Is *he* there?' the Queen asked in their shared native tongue, as if she was asking if a dog had just defiled her throne room.

'Yes. Oliver's here. He is fifty per cent of the equation,' Lia replied in English, with more bravura than she felt.

The Queen cleared her throat, then said in cut-glass English, 'We're ready to announce the wedding. End of the month.'

'But I haven't agreed to it yet!'

'I have,' Oliver said.

Everything in her stilled apart from her eyes,

which locked with Oliver's. What was he doing? Undermining her?

'The announcement will come out today,' her grandmother said crisply. 'We've got to act fast to try and blur any confusion about your "premature honeymoon baby".'

Lia's hand flew to her stomach, as if shielding her child from her grandmother's autocratic dictates. 'You've even got the birth story ready?'

Her grandmother made a sound that most people would have thought unbecoming to a queen. 'That's what happens when a princess makes mistakes. The palace is here to fix them. Now. I've spoken with the Duke and Duchess of Banford, and they're quite willing to host any sort of engagement parties that might be required—'

Oliver coughed... Or was he choking? Whatever it was his face had gone much paler than it had been a moment ago.

'Who are the Duke and Duchess of Banford?' Lia asked.

There was the briefest of pauses—one that gave a microscopic hint that somewhere, lurking beneath all that brusque efficiency, her grandmother might actually be feeling some compassion for her. Or maybe she was smirking. Who knew? They weren't exactly the sort of family to sit around the kitchen table and play board games together.

'As you know, the Duke of Banford holds one of England's most honourable seats...' her grandmother began.

Lia made a face at Oliver that she hoped said *I have no idea what she's on about.*

'Amelia?' Her grandmother gave an impatient tut. 'You do know that the man you had your...*dalliance* with is to become the Duke of Banford one day, don't you?'

Oliver shifted uncomfortably.

Oliver was a member of England's aristocracy? What the hell was this? She felt as if she was being trapped in a vice.

Her eyes began blinking so fast that Oliver looked as if he were caught in the flares of a strobe light. She wasn't completely au fait with the British gentry, but even she knew that the Duke of Banford was a mainstay amongst the establishment...which meant Oliver was, too.

And the Duke was rich.

Very rich.

So this wasn't a 'marry rich to save the poor aristocratic family seat' thing.

What the hell was it, then?

Why hadn't he said anything?

As her grandmother continued to talk, she felt as if the words were impaling her. *Heir... Country seat... Impressive estate...*

The wedding would take place at the Harbour Hotel, as it would keep the 'awkward nature of the event' more low-key. The palace would see to the logistics.

'We've scheduled another talk with the Duke and Duchess to settle the matter in an hour.'

Oliver looked everywhere but at her as her grandmother prattled on about how many guests there would be, which socialite magazine would receive exclusive coverage, and on and on.

Lia's bloodstream turned icy cold. She'd known it. Whatever it was they'd shared had been far too good to go any deeper than the one-night stand they'd agreed on.

Weighted sheets of anger, hurt and confusion

fell over her in enormous canopies, pressing the oxygen from her lungs as each one landed.

Shakily, she began to rise from the picnic seat.

Oliver took hold of her arm. 'Sit down, Lia. Please.'

'Amelia?' Her grandmother's voice broke through the increasingly thick tropical air that normally signalled a rain shower. 'Perhaps you should ask your…*friend* to step away? Or take the phone off speaker. I'd rather not have him listen in on our private conversation?'

'It's hardly private!' Lia snapped back. 'Seeing as he's going to be *family* in a month's time.'

Oliver winced as she ground out 'family' as if it were a bad word.

A low buzzing began in her ears as her grandmother handed the conversation over to one of the press secretaries, who rattled off a series of dates. Today for the engagement announcement, then a press statement detailing their 'love at first sight' meeting at the gala, where their shared passion for charitable events quickly blossomed into something deeper and, as such, led to their swift decision to marry.

When you knew, you knew—that was the long and short of it.

Lia forced herself to look at Oliver. Had she known the instant she met him that she wanted him?

Yes.

That she loved him?

Her insides crumpled. She didn't know. Her family was led by a king and queen more in love with their obligations to The Crown than one another. Her father had let the monarchy—his parents—destroy his marriage and bully his wife into a modern-day banishment which had culminated in a depression so deep he'd sent his five-year-old daughter off to boarding school, where she had spent years aching for something she had never really been able to name because she'd longed for something she had never known. A happy family. Love.

So, no. The one thing she definitely didn't know anything about was love at first sight. And yet here she was, toeing the same line. Fulfilling her royal duty not to embarrass The Crown on behalf of a nation whose moral compass could never be seen to waver.

She trained her eyes on Oliver's, willing them to tell her something—anything to assure her that, whatever happened, they could weather the storm.

He looked every bit as rattled as she did.

And then, as if a switch had been flicked, his entire physique changed. He rolled his shoulders back, straightened his spine. He practically glowed with an aura of control. He looked taller, stronger. Capable. Able to surmount each and every hurdle that the palace might put in their way—which was when it hit her.

Oliver was rising to the challenge.

Rather than wanting to run away to another, even more remote island, like she did, he was squaring off with his past. Confronting a childhood of being forced into a box he'd never wanted to be in. He was doing exactly what she'd told him she wanted from a man. Becoming someone prepared to fight to the death for her.

And suddenly—desperately—she wanted this to work.

They clicked. The reason she'd felt safe with him that one wild night was because they knew exactly what the other was made of. Sugar and spice and everything royal. Well… That was what little princesses were made of. She wasn't entirely sure what prospective dukes were made of, but she had four weeks to find out before she married him. If, of course, they came up with an acceptable game plan.

Because that was what this would be. A game of wits. She and Oliver joining forces to fight The Karolinskan Crown for control of their child.

Lia clicked off the phone whilst the press secretary was still in full flow and fixed Oliver with a look that said, *This is what you're asking to be part of. And by 'this' I mean Crazyville.*

'We can do this,' he said. He took her hands in his and with a soft, kind smile. 'We can do this for our child. We can play their game and win.'

A flicker of belief lit in her chest. It was faint and wary, and a thousand shades of nervous, but he was right. This was bigger than either of them. She wasn't just carrying her child. She was carrying *their* child. And that child's future was worth fighting for as a team.

It was time to be brave.

She looked up into his eyes. 'Do you really want to do this?'

'I really want to do this.'

* * *

Oliver felt both shell-shocked and shot through with single-minded focus.

He was going to get married.

Correction. He was being told to get married, be stripped of his anonymity and likely have zero control over anything beyond his career over the next month.

He should be feeling as though he'd leapt out of the frying pan and into the fire. Lia was from a family like his. Worse, actually, if that phone call was anything to go by. And the fact that he was giving his father another heir meant the pressure would ramp up on him to return home. Assume some of his father's social duties and, while he was there, take care of the estate.

The bulk of the sprawling estate was tenanted out to farmers, but the manor house was every bit as big as any in those 'how the other half lives' series on television he could never quite get himself to watch.

On top of which, arranged marriages had a long and not very successful history in his family. Everyone stayed married because it was what titled people did, but there was no happiness in it. No joy.

But none of it mattered because he was going to be a father, a parent. And with the first woman to make him feel properly alive again in six years.

Lia was tracing her finger round a set of initials that had been carved into the picnic table. Her body language suggested she still wasn't entirely convinced that getting married was the best of ideas. Without looking up at him, she asked, 'Why didn't you tell me you were a duke?'

'I'm not a duke,' he replied. *'Yet,'* he added, more honestly.

He moved round to her side of the table so that she had to look at him. If he wanted transparency from her, he owed her the same. 'I'm sorry I didn't tell you about the duke thing.'

Lia huffed and rolled her eyes, murmuring something about honesty being a fairly useful policy. She was right.

'I don't like being judged by my title,' he said. 'I want people to judge me for who I am.'

'And just who is that, exactly?'

Oliver ached to pull her in. Soothe her defensiveness away. He was feeling as blindsided as she was, but the shock felt surmountable. Something the two of them could face head-on.

'I'm a paediatrician who loves his job, doesn't love the aristocracy, and is insanely happy that we're going to have a baby.'

There was more, of course. Other chapters in his life that had made him the man he was today.

'And what makes you think we'll work…as a couple?' She turned her hands towards herself. 'It's not like you really know me.'

He thought of their shared night of passion. His hands caressing that sweet dip between her ribcage and hip before he slipped his fingers between her legs. How she'd moaned in pleasure when he'd lowered himself into her. How their orgasms had come at the same time and they'd both laughed with disbelief and pleasure.

He knew elements of her. And once again, for the first time in a long time, he was very much looking forward to getting to know her better.

'That's why we're here, eating fish and chips,' he said instead.

She snorted, clearly not pleased. 'You think a meal out exchanging favourite colours and comfort foods makes us a match?'

'No,' he countered. 'I think whatever it is that made two people who don't do one-night stands have one does.'

She looked at him sharply, then covered her face with her hands. He didn't press. If her brain was whirring as fast as his was, she needed the thinking time.

Eventually, she peeked out at him between her fingers. 'What are we going to do?'

'We're going to get married,' he said.

They'd each managed to escape the grip of the past before. They would be able to do it again. And, as his favourite headmaster had told him on that first bewildering day at boarding school, *'You can do anything for ten seconds.'*

He'd done a lot of things for ten seconds, and then another ten, and another. It had taught him that he could withstand almost anything that was thrown at him. But he knew he wanted more than anything to be with the mother of his child, and be there to support them both, as a family. To be a father.

Lia was staring at him. 'How can you sound so certain?'

'Because I like you,' he said honestly. Then,

more to the point, 'And I am not going to leave you stranded in this situation. You didn't get here on your own.' He swallowed against a surge of emotion. 'And I want to be there to raise our child.'

'Don't you want to—?' Again, she stopped herself short, swatting away what looked like her own rush of emotion.

Fall in love? Was that what she was going to ask?

Hell's teeth.

Of course he wanted to love the woman he married. And she was right. He barely knew her. But his hands twitched with a muscle memory that said otherwise. He'd known her body's secret desires well enough. Could he grow to know her heart's?

Time and circumstance were not luxuries they could play with. There was only one way to find out if they were a match. Pour their energies into getting to know one another.

He stood up and gave her a courtly bow, just as his parents had taught him when he'd first met the Queen.

'What do you say we go down to the beach? We can watch the sunset, play another round of Twenty Questions. Do it every hour of every day, if you like. Unless, of course, you have other plans for your evening?'

'Other than preparing my trousseau...not really,' she said with a self-effacing laugh.

'You didn't grow up embroidering your wedding veil for this very moment?' he joked, but instantly knew he'd overstepped the fragile weave of their new relationship as her smile slid into a frown.

Lia swept some strands of hair away from her face before she spoke. Her voice was deadly serious as she said, 'This isn't a fairy tale. You know that marrying me means an end to your quiet, anonymous life, don't you?'

'You're carrying our child. That takes precedence. *You* take precedence.'

A flash of something he couldn't identify flared in her eyes. 'What if I refuse to marry you?'

A blaze of alpha energy shot through him like lightning. There was no chance he would let this second, precious opportunity to become a father be snatched from him.

It took every ounce of self-control to keep his voice level as he looked her in the eye and said, 'I will love our child with every fibre of my being. I will respect you and honour you. We have a connection. You know that. The only question is, are we brave enough to find out if we can make it into something that will last a lifetime?'

Lia's heart was pounding so hard she could barely register her own thoughts, let alone absorb what Oliver had just said.

He'd look after her. He'd love their child. He'd do his best to care for her.

It wasn't exactly the outpouring of love she'd one day hoped for…but perhaps this was better. Mutual respect and understanding.

Instinct was telling her she would instantly have rejected any declaration of love after so little time knowing one another. It would have rung false and given his every move a sheen of dishonesty. Of wanting something other than to accept his responsibility as a parent. The pain of her parents' rejection had never left her, and heartbreak was something she wasn't sure she could endure again.

She looked deep into Oliver's eyes, exploring the rich kaleidoscope of blues framed by pitch-black lashes, and saw something that moved her on a profound level. He already loved their child. In a handful of time—minutes, really — he'd received two huge life bombs. An unexpected pregnancy and decreed-from-above nuptials. Yet somehow he'd managed to absorb the far more pressing truth: they were going to be parents. And his gut response was love.

It shone a completely different light on the future the palace was trying to superimpose on them. If he was strong enough and brave enough to pull his heart out of his chest and put it on his sleeve in this way, he might have the strength to stand up to her family in a way her mother never could.

Did she have the strength to do the same thing?

She looked at him. Really looked at him. His blue eyes were alive with...what was it, exactly? *Presence.* He was here with her—body and soul—asking her if she would take the same risk he was willing to take in order to ensure their child grew up feeling loved.

She tipped her head to the side, feeling stupidly shy, and asked, 'How do you feel about a fiancée who can't cook?'

His eyes lit up. 'So long as you're happy with toasted cheese sandwiches and orange slices, I'm fine with that.'

It wasn't the most obvious way to say, *I'm in. Let's get married*, but in another one of those silent exchanges they both knew what had just happened.

They were going to get married.

They gave the moment some air, then Oliver reached his hand out to hers, his fingers weaving through hers as if they'd done it a thousand times before. The gesture spoke volumes. They were a team now. They were going to get married and have a child.

Was it terrifying?

Absolutely.

Was her gut telling her to run for the hills? Become a hermit living in a cave somewhere?

Not anymore.

She'd never met a man willing to confront what he knew would be a difficult future hand in hand with her.

'I've got an idea,' he said.

She raised her eyebrows and nodded for him to go ahead.

'Let's shelve all talk about weddings and babies for tonight. Carry on with our date.'

Her chest filled with warm gratitude. There was so much going on in her head right now she was almost too frightened to speak. And he was giving each of them space to digest this tectonic shift in their lives.

After the sun had dipped below the horizon they strolled along the beach, throwing one another the odd 'softball' question. Favourite sport. Least favourite food. Favourite spot on the island. But mostly they lapsed into thoughtful silence as each of them let their new reality settle deep into their bones.

Without having talked about it, they ended up at Oliver's house, with the faintest remains of the sunset still pinking up the sky. She let herself really absorb the place. Whilst from the beach the house appeared to be hanging in the trees, it was actually very firmly built into a sharp rising stone bluff dappled with old-growth trees.

'I like how you can see the sunset on this side of the island,' she said as they made their way up a flight of stairs to the kitchen.

'Tired of the sunrise over on your side of the

island, are you?' He stopped mid-step. 'Unless, of course, princesses don't get up that early.' He dropped her a comedic wink to ensure she would know he was kidding.

She rolled her eyes, then said, 'I'll have you know I never sleep. It's all those pesky peas finding their way underneath my mattresses.'

'Mattresses, eh? I only have the one.'

'I remember,' she said airily, a few vivid memories of their night sending a flush to her cheeks.

Oliver's tongue swept along his lips—a clear sign that he remembered their shared night of passion with equal clarity. He ran his index finger along the curve of her cheek. Her breath hitched in her throat as his fingertip reached her lips.

They were halfway between the bedroom and the kitchen. It would be a matter of a few steps to change course and go to his bed.

Oliver abruptly led her into the kitchen. He was right. Tonight was for talking, not confirming what they both already knew. Their sexual chemistry was never going to be a problem.

The kitchen, like the other rooms, was fronted with a long row of floor-to-ceiling retractable glass doors. There was a small native hardwood kitchen table inside, and a much bigger one outside on the covered deck—which, Lia was delighted to see, had two large trees growing through the decking that soared up into the tropical canopy above. The back of the room was a long line of doors.

'I thought there was a cliff back there?'

'Cupboards,' Oliver explained, opening a couple to show her the contents, as if everyone had massive storage areas for food and kitchen implements in their luxury treehouse.

Her version of haute cuisine was pretty much limited to fruit. The staff restaurant at The Island Clinic was staffed by Michelin chefs, and even their casual 'snack food' was on another level.

Beneath three large filament bulbs in the centre of the room a gorgeous sprawl of marble topped a kitchen island, at the centre of which was a lovely fruit bowl. She closed her eyes, imagining what it would be like if she were the type of woman to sweep the bowl off the counter and to replace it with herself.

'Want something to eat?' he asked.

Her eyes flicked open to meet his.

No. She didn't. She wanted him.

He must have seen her hunger for him flare in her eyes and thrown his own reservations into the bonfire, because before she could draw a full breath he was kissing her. Urgently. Possessively. Tenderly.

Their shared energy was urgent and gentle. Generous and hungry. Though their words remained unspoken, they both knew these were precious moments—the ones before the palace descended. There would be staff. Rules. Endless instructions. But this…here and now, before anyone, anywhere, boarded a plane with so much as a solitary fabric swatch…this was their time. Time she wanted to put a glass cloche over and preserve, as if it was the most precious thing in the world.

Though they'd made love before, this time it felt entirely different. As if their bodies were making vows to each other. To care and protect. To adore. To love.

Lia feared drowning in it. Losing herself to the very thing she'd promised herself she'd never do: the Palace's bidding. But Oliver exuded a confidence about their shared future that charged her own faltering belief in herself. This was about *them*, not Karolinska, or his family's title. Just the two of them—and, of course, the child she was now carrying.

With each caress, every kiss he tenderly dropped on her belly, she felt as though she was absorbing his silent promises.

We'll be different. We won't let them change us. We won't let them take away the happiness we want for our child. For our family.

As the energy between them grew more charged, more intimate, she finally allowed herself to give in fully to her own body's longing to offer Oliver the same silent vows.

What the palace didn't know wouldn't hurt them. Would it?

CHAPTER SEVEN

'You ready?'

'Not *camera*-ready,' Oliver replied, giving his hair a ruffle that made him look even less so.

Nope. Not so much as a smile. *Okay...* So someone wasn't pleased about the palace photographer tagging along for this 'spontaneous' sailing trip.

'There she is.' Lia pointed to the end of the dock to her sailing boat.

The teak-decked *Island Dreamer* had two huge masts, a dozen rigging lines—at least that was what Oliver thought they were called—and, slightly disconcertingly, only one visible flotation device.

'You're not planning on drowning me at sea, are you?' Oliver joked as he looked at the impressive sailing boat, then back at his bride-to-be.

Bride-to-be.

He shook his head. What a difference one

night of passion with a princess made. Well…
One night, a month's break and then several
more nights, during which both of their worlds
had changed completely.

All the things that needed to happen on a
practical level—like actually discussing their
Harbour Hotel wedding—had yet to happen. It
was as if discussing it would make it real, without time to take a breath and think about what
they wanted, and they were both feeling bowled
over by the Karolinskan palace-led reality.

They'd agreed to sit down and talk about
it every night after work. And they had met.
Only there hadn't been much talking. Without
so much as a whisper of a decision about what
type of flowers they'd like, or what flavour of
cake they wanted, they'd end up in bed. Which,
to be fair, was no bad thing. It was not entirely
useful when it came to answering the palace's
never-ending stream of emails…but it seemed
to be the one thing they could cling to that was
solely theirs.

Today, however, was different. Today was
'palace-sanctioned.' The family's official photographer had arrived. Tomorrow the wedding
planning team would set up camp at the same

hotel where they'd had the gala. It was where Oliver and Lia had met, and it had been deemed 'the most suitable' location.

Today was their first 'accidentally on purpose' photo shoot, and Lia was as skittish as a highly bred racehorse. As beautiful as ever, but…less accessible. And he was feeling the loss of their shared connection. If it was a sign of what was to come for them—a withdrawal of her affection whenever the palace was involved—he wasn't entirely sure their future would be as rosy as he'd hoped.

But he pushed his concerns about shared custody and having to move to Karolinska to ensure he'd have a relationship with his child to the side. They weren't there yet, and with any luck they never would be.

Lia laughed at his feeble quip, but her eyes remained on the sailing boat. 'Consider yourself lucky. I don't take just anyone out on her.'

'No? Why not?'

'It's my happy place. Once that tether's undone, it's just me, myself and I.'

Her expression remained the same, but the ghost of a shadow darkened those light blue eyes of hers—as if she were remembering countless other places that made her sad.

Oliver winced in sympathy as an instinctual tug of protectiveness leapt to the fore. Though they'd not spoken about it explicitly, he knew their childhoods, although hundreds of miles apart, had been remarkably similar. Hers had compelled her to choose the life of a loner, to keep the pain at bay, whereas he had thrown himself into the fray. He had always loved bringing joy and happiness to others.

A niggling thought surfaced. Had *all* his happiness been by proxy?

She caught him looking at her. His expression must have still been caught in the wince, because she added a mischievous, 'Don't worry. Only people I genuinely like are allowed aboard. There are more flotation vests down in the cabin.'

Her eyes left his and travelled to the two sails bound tight against the masts. One was a deep blue, the other brilliant white. The colours of the Karolinskan flag. So there was some national pride in her. But not any sense of freedom.

He wondered if there would ever be a day

when the two could be combined. When she could do her royal duty, but also feel she was living the best version of herself. He stopped short of wondering the same thing for himself. The family seat had always felt like a mausoleum to him. He was dreading the inevitable question his brief chats with his parents were building towards.

When will you come home?

He scanned the length of the boat until his eyes hit the stern, and there it was, the royal family's crest emblazoned on a blue and white flag, fluttering in the light breeze, giving the odd snap to attention, as if it was aware Lia was about to board.

His own family's crest wasn't dissimilar. A lion, an axe and a dragon were all shared symbols. Things that ruled with might. Hers, however, beneath the golden crown, also bore the scales of justice.

She caught him examining the crest. 'Hope you like it. They'll be stitching it into your boxers before long. "Property of the Karolinskan Crown."'

His clipped laugh matched the dark humour

of her comment. Just the reminder he needed that they weren't alone.

He swung his duffel bag onto the deck of the boat and said, 'I hope the clothes I've brought please The Crown.'

He'd been running late, so hadn't given much thought to the clothes he'd stuffed into it. His mother would have been horrified. She planned the look of their family portraits for months beforehand, so in fairness his boxers—at home, at least—really did symbolically bear the Banford crest sometimes. But the rest of the year he was plain old Oliver Bainbridge. And he liked it that way.

As if a knife had been abruptly shunted between his ribs, Oliver absorbed the reality that the minute he became Lia's husband all of that would change...

Too late, he realised that he was frowning, and that Lia had noticed.

She bit down on her lower lip and gave it a chew, as if debating whether or not to tell him something. Clearly something that had been weighing on her.

It had only been a few days since they'd learnt about her pregnancy, but so much had happened since then. Press releases had been written and lists of the things they had to do to make the 'party line' from the Karolinska press office bear weight had been issued. Which was why, after another full day in surgery for Lia and full office hours at the hospital for him, they were down here at the private yacht club for a photo shoot.

It was meant to look as if they were casual snaps of the couple caught by surprise, but Oliver was swiftly learning how pre-planned the rest of his life might be.

He reached out and touched Lia's arm, warm with the late-afternoon sun. 'Are you all right, Lia?'

'Absolutely.'

Her voice was light, but there was something behind it. Something she wasn't saying.

He took her hand in his and tipped his head towards the entrance of the small yacht club, where the photographer was already standing, multiple lenses slung round his neck. 'We don't have to do this.'

'Yes,' she replied with a *This is precisely what I warned you about* smile, 'we do.'

She gently tugged her hand free and made a move to board the boat.

She turned suddenly, her body language radiating defensiveness. 'Unless you're having second thoughts?'

Her tone was sharp, remonstrative in a way he wouldn't have expected from someone who was almost literally in the same boat as him.

'I'll never have second thoughts about being a father to my child.'

Her entire body grew taut with coiled energy. He'd clearly said the wrong thing. But with a photographer a handful of metres away, this wasn't the time to have it out, so he stuffed his hands in his pockets, his fingers catching on the small square box he hadn't told Lia about.

It wasn't a traditional engagement ring. It was an eternity ring. A symbol he hoped would remind her, every time she looked at it over the coming months, that the child she was carrying would link them together for ever.

She glanced at her watch. 'C'mon. Let's get this over with.'

An hour later the photographer had what he needed and they sailed out of the protected harbour area and beyond the island. Though the shoreline was still within view, the holiday-makers on the beach appeared as tiny figurines on a film set representing yet another perfect day on St Victoria. The only thing missing was the happy atmosphere that Lia had intimated would exist once they'd been 'caught' in an embrace as they prepared the boat for departure.

She'd changed clothes and poses three times in order to give the palace photographer plenty of material to work with. Shorts and a T-shirt. A sundress dotted with poppies. And now a pair of figure-hugging navy pedal-pushers with a blue and white scarf standing in as a belt and a white shirt, knotted at her belly button, sleeves rolled up to her elbows and, a bit disconcertingly, unbuttoned to that sweet spot just at the arc of her breasts.

It was teasing at the memories Oliver had of last night…giving her nipples hot, swift licks, then drawing them into his mouth for another swirl and a light rasp of his teeth as she groaned her approbation.

There was no such sensuality in the atmosphere today, let alone the primal hunger they'd shared. The past hour had felt impersonal in a way that had surprised him. Lia had directed him, *sotto voce*, to kiss her shoulder as she looked out into the middle distance, or to turn his face in a particular direction so the light was right when they looked into one another's eyes before untying the yacht from the dock.

Now, with the sails loosed from the masts and easily catching the breeze, the boat looked utterly resplendent. Free. He looked at Lia, standing at the steering wheel with the wind in the strands of white-blonde hair that hadn't been caught in the knot at the nape of her neck, and he saw the woman he'd originally met at the charity function. One too aware of all eyes being on her. Of judgement being cast without consideration for her feelings. She seemed trapped in a cage.

He looked over to the small speedboat that had followed them out of the harbour. It sounded its horn and then turned back to shore.

When he looked at Lia again, and their eyes met, he wasn't sure who he was looking at. Not the woman who had danced in his arms and kissed him on the beach. But nor was it the *Look that way*, media-savvy, aloof princess she'd been the past hour.

A part of him wanted to pull her into his

arms and tell her that as long as they did things together—as a team—they'd be fine. But this photo shoot had unleashed an uncertainty in him that he was finding hard to shake. He felt as though he'd been pushed a cool arm's length away from Princess Amelia and he didn't like it.

He wanted Lia, who had walked with him in the rain last night, talking about her surgeries. The woman who'd made love to him in the outdoor shower before seductively slipping under the bedcovers and beckoning him with impossible-to-resist bedroom eyes.

Not this picture-perfect bride-to-be. Laughing on cue. Colouring slightly as he cupped her cheek in his hand. Lips virtually frozen as they pressed to his for a slow-motion peck while the shutters of the palace camera whirred and clicked away.

He forced himself to backpedal. His own annual Christmas, Easter and summer holiday portraits were hardly bursts of spontaneous familial affection. He'd been lucky in that the nannies and boarding schools his parents had chosen for him had been a welcome substitute. He had plenty of friends and mentors from school that he was still in touch with to this day.

Perhaps Lia hadn't had even that. Her parents were divorced. From what he could gather she rarely spoke to her father, and she hadn't so much as mentioned her mother. She'd eagle-eyed a fellow boarding school kid in him, so had clearly done her own stint there, and then, of course, boot camp with the Karolinskan army. That wouldn't have been a touchy-feely thing, even for a princess.

And yet, warrior that she was, the palace still clearly wielded enough power to make her bend to their will to an extent—and that was where the heart of his uncertainty lay.

He jammed his hands in his pockets, and once again his fingertips butted against the small square box. He'd planned to slip the ring on Lia's finger back at the yacht club, suspecting the photographer would be looking for some sort of sparkle befitting a princess, but it hadn't felt right. In the same way staying in England and following his parents' model of living by the rules of tradition hadn't felt right.

A niggle of discomfort wedged between his conscience and his discomfort with Lia over the past hour. He'd left the life he'd been 'born to live' thousands of miles away, just as Lia had.

But now that they were going to be parents running away wasn't an option. They had to find a shared strength that would shield their child from repeating the pattern.

'Oliver?'

He turned as Lia waved to get his attention.

'Could you help me with this sail?'

He frowned and apologised. 'Sorry. Away with the fairies.' He looked at the sail. 'Should you be hoisting that? In your condition?'

'I'm not made of bone china. I'm pregnant,' she said, visibly offended.

'I know... I just thought maybe you should take things easy.'

'I'm not going to take to my bed for the next eight months, if that's what you're thinking.' Her eyes blazed with indignation, then lowered to half-mast as she inspected him, no doubt wondering if marrying him was the last thing she should do.

He wanted to defend himself when suddenly, just like that, he saw her taut, emotionally withdrawn behaviour for what it really was. Frustration with not having a say in her own life. An ache for exactly the same thing he wanted: a normal, happy life.

She must have sensed his empathy because her expression softened. 'Sorry. I'm not really good at being told what to do.'

'I get it,' he said.

'I know. Of all the people in the world who would get it, you are one of them.' She gave a self-effacing laugh and threw him an apologetic look. 'I feel like you see right into my brain sometimes.'

'No.' He shook his head. 'I see right into this.' He pointed at her heart.

She took his hand and laid it on her chest until, sure enough, he felt her heart's rapid cadence through the light fabric of her top.

'I promise I'll be careful. That I'll protect this little one.' She moved their hands to her belly.

They shared a smile that instantly swept his fears away. There she was. Lia the Princess who didn't want to be a princess. The woman who wanted to be a mother...and, hopefully, a wife.

'Here.' He took the line from her and tugged the sail up. 'Think of me as your chief galley man.'

She laughed and said, 'You'd be making lunch if that was the case. How about first mate?'

'Sounds good.' He tied the rope off under her instructions and gave her a salute.

She feigned wiping sweat off her brow and gave him a sheepish smile. 'Sorry if I've been vile. I hate photo shoots.' She shot him a playful smirk. 'And we're going to have to work on your happy-go-lucky look. You looked stiff as board!'

She cackled, then, as if she were a balloon that had unexpectedly popped, suddenly deflated.

'That was awful,' she said. 'You're going to walk away before the month is over, aren't you?'

He shook his head. 'I'll never walk away. You have my word on that.'

She sought his eyes for any hint of wavering. Obviously finding none, she leant in to give him a sweet, soft kiss that filled him with a honeyed warmth.

'I'm sorry I was a pain,' she whispered against his lips. 'I'm not used to someone having my back.'

That admission spoke volumes. Just as he'd built an enormous fortress round his heart after his ex had had her abortion, Lia kept people at arm's length because it was safer than risking the disappointment of being let down.

Brick by brick, she was opening up his fortress.

Millimetre by millimetre, she was letting him in.

He pulled her to him, one hand on the small of her back, one hand cupping her cheek, and kissed her again. More deeply this time. More meaningfully.

I'm here for you, the kisses said. *You are not alone. You'll never be alone again.*

Eventually, they drew apart, the demands of the boat taking precedence over their urge to let the rest of the world melt away.

'Want to teach me how this thing works?' he asked.

They spent a companionable hour or so, working their way through all the boating terminology. And between learning about winches, pushpins, transoms and jammers, he became aware that their bodies organically sought each other's.

The light brush of a hand… Their legs pressing together when they sat side by side… Their eyes catching and heat passing between them as if they were actually sharing energy…

They were far out enough that they also saw a lot of wildlife. Dolphins…some porpoises. Even a turtle or two.

'Ever seen a manatee?' he asked.

She shook her head. 'They're usually in the mangroves, and I tend to stick to the boat rather than the dinghy.'

He looked for and clocked the small RIB attached to the back of the boat. 'Do you ever use it?

She shook her head. 'Not really. I prefer the power of the wind to motorised power.'

'It's definitely more peaceful this way.'

She tipped her head to his shoulder and they stayed like that for a while, her hair occasionally tickling his cheek, their little fingers touching, then linking. They'd be all right, Oliver thought. There would be bumps and troughs along the way, but…they'd be all right.

'Now,' Lia said after they'd brought the boat around to a quieter side of the island, away from the tourist beaches. She turned a knob on the control panel and pointed at the speaker built into the console. 'Are you ready to learn the radio lingo?'

'Absolutely.' Oliver gave her a crisp salute. 'At your service, Captain.'

She grinned, the bridge of her nose wrinkling just enough to give him a glimpse of what she might have looked like as a little girl, before her parents' divorce. Happy, light, carefree. He made a silent vow to provide her with a future where she could honour that little girl. Give her a second chance to forge a new life for herself and, of course, for their own child.

'Oliver—' Lia's expression changed as she turned up the volume on the radio.

'What?'

'Listen.'

He focused in on the voices on the radio. 'It sounds like a distress call.'

'It is. It's the coastguard. They're on the far side of the island and they...' She paused and leant in to listen. 'It's kayakers. They've got caught in the currents and ended up some-where around here. In the mangroves, I think. It sounds like one of them needs urgent medi-cal attention.'

'Can we get there?' He looked up at the vast

sails, knowing there was no chance they'd get into the thickly forested inlets.

'We can in that.' She pointed at the RIB.

Lia's military training kicked into high gear. She was relieved to note that Oliver worked swiftly and efficiently.

'Two years in a paediatric A&E,' he explained, when she asked if he'd had any emergency training.

'Hopefully you won't need it,' she said grimly as they anchored the boat.

They lowered the sails, tied them off, then quickly got the RIB into the water.

'Do you know the mangroves?' she asked.

He nodded in the affirmative. 'I've taken my kayak in there a lot.'

'You direct, then,' Lia said, taking up a post at the motor.

As they fastidiously made their way through the maze, eyes peeled for the kayakers, they heard shouting.

Nothing prepared them for what they saw.

Two young women—maybe in their late teens—were in a double kayak. One of the girls was screaming and waving her hands at Lia and

Oliver. The second was lying face-down in the small area between the seats, her paddle slipping into the water.

'Barracudas!' screamed the girl. 'We were watching the barracudas jump and then one hit Stephanie!'

Lia's vision clicked into slow-motion frames of information.

The injured girl, Stephanie, had an open wound on her left side, in the gap between the front and back pads of her flotation device. Her lung was visible through her ribs.

After ensuring that the fish were gone, Oliver jumped out of their RIB and began tying the girls' kayak to it. He waded through the waist-deep water and, after pulling on a pair of clean surgical gloves, asked for a moment's silence.

When Lia heard the gurgle indicating a puncture in Stephanie's lung, her first thought was that they were moments away from calling a time of death.

'How long ago did this happen?' she heard Oliver ask.

'Ten minutes ago, maybe?' the frightened girl answered, tears openly pouring down her cheeks.

'What's your name?' Lia asked, her emergency medical training finally clicking into gear, as Oliver's already had.

'Mary.'

'Okay, Mary. Let's get you aboard the RIB.'

Oliver asked Lia for the first aid kit they'd brought along. It was a proper military EMT run bag that she'd used back in her training days, and she'd never been more glad of her precautionary measures to keep it rather than just the customary plasters and paracetamol.

'What's faster?' Lia asked Oliver. 'Getting to shore or sailing back round to the harbour?'

'We can take the RIB in through the mangroves. There's a small docking area not far from here.'

'Can a helicopter land there?'

'Yes. You ring the rescue crew and I'll get Stephanie into the RIB for a needle decompression.'

Lia nodded her agreement. If the injury had happened an hour ago, the girl would have had only a three per cent chance of survival. As things stood, they were at the beginning of the so-called 'golden hour'. They had about fifty minutes to ensure she would survive.

After Oliver had put several large bandages round the open wound, protecting it for the transfer, Lia asked Mary to hold the phone, which was on speaker mode, so she could speak to the coastguard while they gently transferred Stephanie to the RIB.

'She's suffering from a tension pneumothorax,' Lia explained to the woman on the end of the phone.

'What does that mean?' Mary wailed.

As Lia spoke to the emergency services, Oliver explained to Mary that the trauma to Stephanie's lung had trapped air in her pleural cavity—the space between the lungs—and that they had to release it in order to ensure the rest of the body received oxygen.

It was more complicated than that, but Lia appreciated Oliver's attempt to simplify the complicated-sounding situation. The pleural cavity, once filled with air, would cause Stephanie's left lung to collapse, which would then put pressure on her heart, reducing cardiac output, which would make breathing next to impossible and induce tachycardia. Surviving the domino effect of an untreated pneumothorax was impossible.

Half listening to Oliver as she spoke with the coastguard, Lia was impressed with the quick efficiency with which he both worked and talked. He didn't use vocabulary that would alienate Mary. His voice was calm and soothing. He was someone you would trust in an emergency. Someone you would entrust with your child.

'Which hospital?' the woman on the end of the phone asked.

'The Island Clinic,' Lia said.

At the same time Oliver said, 'St Victoria.'

'We have a landing pad—'

Again their voices overlapped.

An ominous sound came from Stephanie's lung. 'You choose,' Oliver said.

There was no doubt that any more time wasted was at this poor girl's peril.

The operator chose for them. 'There's a helicopter already en route to The Island Clinic with a VIP patient in it.'

Time was not their friend. And Lia had no idea what the patient on the helicopter needed. Her hesitation spoke volumes.

The emergency operator said, 'After the drop-off it can come and collect you, but it would be faster to bring her to the hospital. Is that acceptable?'

'Very,' Lia confirmed.

While the facilities at The Island Clinic were well beyond first rate, St Victoria was a great local hospital. It also had an emergency room, and it was closer to the hotel which had its name emblazoned on the girls' kayak. More importantly, this was no time to play 'My Clinic's Better Than Your Hospital'.

'What's a tension pneumonia?' Mary asked, as if absolutely nothing Oliver had said had registered.

She was shivering, the shock of the incident clearly taking root.

'Pneumothorax,' Oliver quietly corrected, handing her an emergency foil blanket, despite the heat of the day.

He began his explanation again in a low voice, so Lia could finish up her phone call with the emergency services.

Lia pocketed the phone after the rendezvous point had been confirmed and they'd settled Stephanie onto her uninjured right side.

'Why aren't we going?' Mary fretted.

'We just need to do this quick release of

trapped oxygen and then we'll be off,' Oliver explained.

Lia handed him an eight-millimetre fourteen-gauge needle. His eyes caught hers.

'The military recommends the longer length,' she explained.

Military training had not only toughened her up, it had given her access to learn extensive emergency medical treatment, including the latest methods of pre-hospital pneumothorax treatment. Unfortunately, gunshot wounds and stabbings were part and parcel of active duty—and, more to the point, precisely why the palace had forbidden her from serving in a conflict zone.

'No flash chamber,' Oliver commented as he swept an alcohol disinfectant pad over the spot between Stephanie's second intercostal space and the mid-clavicular line where the catheter needle would release the trapped air.

'No need for this type of injury,' she said. 'It means you don't have to think about it.'

He made a noise, as if he was impressed by the forethought, and then got to work. A swift, accurate needle decompression was the only thing that would save this girl's life.

Within seconds the sound every doctor wanted to hear mixed with the softly cadenced noise of water lapping against the side of the boat: the hiss of released air.

Oliver removed the needle but left the catheter in place. Lia took the needle from him and secured it in a proper disposal box. She handed him some tape and he secured the catheter, so that it would continue to act as a valve for any trapped air. They might have to repeat the process, but for now it seemed to have done the trick. Long enough, at least, for them to get the girl to the air ambulance, where she would be able to get an oxygen mask and other critical assistance.

'Are you ready for me to start the engine?' Lia asked, not wanting to literally rock the boat if he needed it to be still.

'Yes, we're good.' He gave her a nod, his eyes still on Stephanie, two fingers pressed to her pulse point.

She noted a small flush of colour begin to return to the girl's cheeks. They were out of the woods for now.

An hour later, having hitched a ride with the air ambulance crew back to the hospital, Mary,

Lia and Oliver were sitting side by side in the waiting room of the St Victoria Hospital, waiting to hear a full report from the emergency team who were in with Stephanie now.

They saw a couple rush in towards the main desk, their faces frantic with worry, and heard them ask after Mary Thewliss and Stephanie Thomas.

'That'll be Mum and Dad, then,' Oliver said, already rising.

Mary ran to them and fell into their arms, crying again, telling them how frightening it had been, and how two people had come to help. She turned and pointed them out.

Lia and Oliver crossed to the couple, who introduced themselves as Stephanie's parents. 'We're ever so grateful you saved her life.'

'Well,' Oliver said humbly, 'we got her to the right place anyhow.'

Alive, Lia thought grimly.

After an incident such as Stephanie had been through, a patient would always end up here, but if they hadn't been as close as they had…

She shuddered, not wanting to go there.

'Will she live?' Stephanie's mother asked, barely waiting for an answer as she turned on her husband, berating him for letting the girls go out in the kayak.

Just as quickly, she began explaining their life story. They were in St Victoria on holiday, to celebrate the girls' graduation from college. The two of them were best friends—had been since they were young. Couldn't separate them for love nor money. They were even going to the same university. But the girls found everything interesting—*too* interesting—and this was what came of exploring unknown territories. She *knew* they should have stayed in the UK and gone camping. Inland. Where it was safe.

Lia was impressed with the compassion Oliver displayed as he listened and nodded, assuring Stephanie's parents that, pending any unforeseen complications, their daughter would be absolutely fine and have one heck of a story to tell.

Then, after the arrival of the team of doctors who had been cleaning and closing Stephanie's wounds, Oliver and Lia were free to go.

'What do you want to do about the boat?' Oliver asked.

Lia squinted out at the setting sun. Night

came early in the tropics and, given how much adrenaline they'd shot in the past couple of hours, she wasn't up for night sailing.

'I can borrow a trailer from the yacht club and pick up the dinghy tomorrow. I'll go out and get the boat after work.'

'I can help,' Oliver volunteered.

She was about to protest, to say she could sort it, but then she reminded herself that this was the man who had put up with her being completely impossible during the photo shoot.

As if Oliver had seen her hesitation—the mix of longing and fear—he gave her arm a squeeze, then took a step back as if to give her room to think, 'You know, I'm actually spending tomorrow at The Island Clinic. I could…if you're happy for me to drive you home…stay there? Maybe try your famed takeaway?'

She was ready to protest again. So far they'd only gone into the clinic grounds under the cover of darkness, and had never appeared as a couple.

She was about to say no when she experienced a lightbulb moment.

Perhaps one of the reasons she found it difficult to make friends was because she'd become too used to protecting her privacy. Too quick to push people away before they could do the same to her. She'd never let previous boyfriends come to her flat, let alone the palace, always finding one excuse or another to keep them at arm's length. Oliver had yet to come to her little cottage on the clinic's grounds.

Her new reality dug its fingers in. If she wanted this marriage to work, she was going to have to find a way to trust Oliver. The palace was clearly on board. Oliver was obviously over the moon about becoming a father. So what else did she need?

Love.

It was what she'd ached for her entire life. Someone to lean on through thick and thin, and not to fear the moment when they stepped away.

She looked at Oliver as he excused himself to sign a couple of papers before they left the hospital. He was kind. Smart. Funny. He definitely fancied her. And he could read her mind. If there was anyone in the world she could fall in love with, he would be a top candidate.

So why wasn't she head over heels right now?

Fear.

Bone-deep terror that he was only marrying her out of duty, for the chance to have an heir for his own family seat, that one day the palace would do to him what it had done to her mother—drive him away, never to return.

Before she could let the ever-increasing mountain of fears consume her, he finished his paperwork, came over and gave her shoulder a squeeze. 'So? What do you think? Shall we head over to your side of the island tonight?'

Crikey. He really could read minds.

She gave a slightly over-enthusiastic nod and said, 'Sounds good.'

'You look thrilled, but you don't *sound* thrilled,' Oliver observed with an easy laugh.

She elbowed him and tried to tease away her nerves with a white lie. 'How will we explain everything in the morning?'

'Well...' He tapped his chin, as if he was giving the matter some serious thought. 'We could tell them I'm actually working for the Karolinskan Secret Service and I'm part of your new Nocturnal Protection Team.'

She laughed. The tight knot of worry in her chest loosened. She could do this. *They* could do this.

The arrival of a brightly coloured shuttle bus caught her eye. It was the free shuttle The Island Clinic provided to bring nurses and doctors and other staff the forty-minute ride between facilities.

As they were without a vehicle, she pointed towards the bus and said, 'Shall we take my horse and carriage? It's got to be home by midnight.'

'With pleasure.'

As if he'd done it a thousand times, he reached for her hand. Her initial instinct was to tug it away. Keep what was happening between them private. But the press release and photos of them as a 'happy couple' would be out the next morning...

So she gave his hand a squeeze and together they boarded the bus.

CHAPTER EIGHT

'THIS TILAPIA IS AMAZING.'

Lia nodded, her mouth dancing with the myriad of flavours in yet another success from The Island Clinic restaurant. 'Not a bad place to get takeaway, is it?'

Oliver nodded his agreement, took another bite, then asked, 'Do you never eat in the restaurant?'

She shook her head. 'No'.

His eyes widened. 'Why not? Don't you like eating with your friends?'

Well, this was awkward. She didn't really have any.

She tried for a jokey response. 'You know how it is...trying to fight a reputation for being a picky princess.'

'What?' he said with mock shock. 'You were lying about the peas the other day?'

She quirked her head to the side, not connecting the dots.

'The other day,' he said, trying to jog her memory. 'You made a comment about the peas underneath your mattresses.'

Before she could answer, he put his fork down on the gorgeous wood table situated in the private garden behind her house.

'Lia,' he said. 'I will never know exactly what your childhood was like, but I do know what it's like to grow up having everyone expect you to act a certain way.'

A welcome surge of connection sent a warmth through her. How did he always know the perfect thing to say?

'It's exhausting, isn't it? Trying to behave one way to counter what you think everyone is saying about you.'

'It's why I moved here,' he admitted cheerfully. 'It's been bliss being plain old Dr Bainbridge.'

She scrunched her nose. 'But you're not plain old Dr Bainbridge, are you?'

'To my patients I am,' he said. 'And to my friends. There really aren't very many people who think of me as the future Duke of Banford—except perhaps my parents and maybe some cousins.' He sat back in his chair and gave her a decidedly wicked smile. 'I hope *you* think of me as something slightly less formal than Dr Bainbridge.'

'Only slightly?' she teased.

'Dramatically,' he conceded, and then, more thoughtfully, 'Seriously, Lia. Apart from the obvious—you, me and the baby—I don't want you to think about me as a duke or even a doctor. I want you to think of me as the man you met at the gala.'

'Gosh,' she sighed. 'All I've *ever* wanted is for people to think of me as a doctor.'

'From what I hear round the clinic, you've got exactly what you wanted.'

The words weren't meant to wound her, but they did.

He was right. Here at the clinic Dr Amelia Trelleburg, neurosurgeon, was the only side of herself she'd ever let people see. Meticulous, serious, solely focused on her work.

She'd been thrilled to be hand-picked by the clinic's founder, Dr Nate Edwards. He'd brought in specialists from around the world and had created an egalitarian environment where no one peacocked or demanded special treatment. They were all here to pour their energies into their shared passion: healing people. And she loved it.

She'd thought that was all that would ever be needed from her—her skills. But three years in she saw that all she'd succeeded in doing was compartmentalising herself. Locking herself away during her non-working hours so that she never had to risk being rejected. Except, of course, for that one night of lust-filled bliss with Oliver.

The truth exploded inside her like a healing tonic. She was the only one standing in the way of receiving the love she so desperately craved.

She looked at Oliver, so kind and generous. Patient. The man was made of patience. And she'd be a fool to test its outer limits.

Right. She could do this. She could be honest. Open. Share private stuff.

She put down her fork and looked him in the eye, forcing herself to think of the 'Amelia trivia' she'd only ever imagined telling her husband.

'Did you know I trained with the military but my family refused to let me serve?'

He nodded.

That wasn't exactly a huge revelation, so she

added. 'I was furious at first. So angry I actually considered cutting and dying my hair and going off to battle in disguise.'

He smiled at the thought. 'Did you have the disguise planned?'

'No,' she admitted. 'It was a pretty short-lived rebellion.'

It had been minutes, really. Seconds… She'd given in quite quickly. Too quickly for someone who claimed to want control of her own life.

'What changed?' Oliver asked, steering her away from darker thoughts.

'I found neurosurgery.'

'That hadn't been your chosen field?'

'Not initially. It was combat medicine.'

'That explains your incredible first-aid run bag.' He smiled and gave her a fist-bump.

She giggled with childlike delight. No one fist-bumped princesses. She could see herself getting into this sharing and caring thing. With Oliver, anyway.

And that's the whole point, you numbskull. He's your safe place.

'What is it about neurosurgery that you love?' he asked.

'Giving someone back the power to make

their own decisions,' she answered without a moment's hesitation.

Helping people at their most vulnerable— when their crucial decision-making 'machine' was faulty—was an incredible honour. The people who trusted her to perform surgery on them humbled her on a daily basis. If she could build on this…invest the same amount of trust in Oliver as her patients invested in her…they would be invincible.

Their eyes met and locked, and in that moment Lia felt nothing but possibility blossom between the pair of them. Her hand swept to her stomach, and when she looked up she saw his eyes had followed the movement.

'Want to touch?'

He reached across and she put his hand on her belly, resting her hand over his.

They shared the moment in silence and then, naturally, their hands slid apart and they both sat back in their chairs.

'What about you?' she asked. 'Why did you pick paediatrics?'

His expression sobered, then lightened with the thoughtfulness she'd seen in him before. 'A bit like you, I think. I wanted to give children a sense of safety in a place that can be scary. Like boarding school.'

Lia shuddered. '*Bleurgh.* I hated boarding school. Didn't you?'

He shook his head. 'No. Total opposite.'

He gave her a look that said, *I'm going to share something with you that I don't tell most people.*

'It was so much easier for me to be away from my parents than with them. I love them, because they're my parents, but they do not love being parents—and, as a result, they don't really know how to love me.'

Lia sucked in a sharp breath. How awful. It was a different scenario from her own.

Oliver gave her arm a squeeze, as if she was the one who needed consoling and said, 'I don't know why, but I never took it personally. My parents lack…' He looked out into the starlit sky beyond the palms fringing the garden, as if it would provide him with the perfect word. 'They lack the *comfort* that should come from loving someone. Being loved. It's as if they think loving me would make them vulnerable. Weak… So, believe me, I thought boarding school was great. It wasn't just a home away from home. It *was* home. And as I grew older I always saw it as my job to make sure the littler kids felt welcome, too. Not everyone wanted to be away from home as much as I did, but there were a lot of kindred spirits there.'

'I'm so sorry.'

'Don't be. Honestly.' Oliver's expression was genuine. 'I really was better off there.'

Lia had absolutely no idea how he could have emerged from such a cold upbringing as warm and kind as he was. Her parents' marriage had been an unmitigated disaster, but somewhere in there—way back when—she knew it had been founded on love.

When interference from the palace had eventually torn them apart, her father had been drained of any fight he'd once had. And with that loss any love he'd had for Lia had also drained away. She almost literally felt the room turn icy whenever she entered one and saw him there.

A sudden insight into how painful her parents' marital breakdown must have been for her father came to her. Perhaps he hadn't sent Lia to boarding school because he'd hated her.

Maybe he'd pushed her away because she'd reminded him of the man he'd used to be.

A rush of affection for her father strained against her heart. Thanks to Oliver's birthright, Lia was going to have a palace-sanctioned chance to have the family her father never could. She wondered if reaching out to him might be the right thing to do, or if her happiness would only make him angrier.

Lia put the idea to Oliver.

He thought for a moment, as she was learning he always did, then said, 'As long as you feel you're strong enough for the possibility that he might not want the same thing you do, I'd say it's worth the risk. And remember you've got me in your corner.'

He did a little boxing move to back the comment up.

'I wish I'd met you years ago,' she blurted.

Something passed through Oliver's eyes that she couldn't identify. A similar wish? Or something brighter that spoke to their shared future.

'That would've been nice,' he said finally.

'I'm sorry your parents didn't make you feel happy at home,' she continued, wanting him to know that she got it. She understood the pain.

'I think it's amazing that you made lemonade out of lemons. I wish I could've done the same. I'd give anything to have a second chance to try and fix it.'

'Hey…' Oliver soothed. 'We all have different sets of clay to work with, and you did what you could with yours. What happened between your parents had nothing to do with you. It's important to look at the positive things in your life. It seems to me you're pretty happy here. You've got your boat. You obviously love your work. You've got me.' He grinned, then turned serious. 'Don't wish away the things you *do* have for things that are out of your control.'

He was right, of course. But common sense was not a fix for a little girl's dreams of a happy childhood.

'I am grateful for everything I have. Truly. I know so many people have it much worse than me. But…there are a couple of things I still wish for,' she said, in a small voice she barely recognised.

'Like what?'

'I wish that we could've got engaged the normal way, for one.' She shot him an apologetic smile.

'What's "normal" these days?' Oliver countered. 'Do you know how many people hunger for exactly what you have? The media at your fingertips… A job at an exclusive clinic… A palace to go home to for the holidays…'

She barked out a laugh, remembering the long list of public appearances that her holidays required. They were more like working holidays than actual breaks. 'If only they knew the reality.'

'Oh, c'mon.' He nudged her toe with his. 'Even though it didn't get a storybook start, life with me isn't going to be that awful. I promise.'

She grinned at him. As far as arranged marriages went…he was right. 'I suppose you're not so bad. Insofar as blokes who live in a treehouse go.'

'Hey! That's our family home you're speaking about,' Oliver protested, his broad smile betraying the pride he felt in his home.

The comment jarred. They hadn't discussed that.

She was about to say she actually preferred the guaranteed privacy of the clinic's grounds, but he looked so contented. So peaceful about the future that had been foisted on him. Which did beg the question…

'If I'd told you I was pregnant and I wasn't a princess…would you still want to marry me?'

'With every fibre of my being,' Oliver replied without hesitation. 'That's our child you're carrying. So I'm in. All the way. And listen, seriously…if you don't like the treehouse we'll live somewhere else. If you've had enough of St Victoria, we'll find another island. If you don't—'

'No! Stop!' Lia protested, giggles forming like champagne bubbles in her throat. 'I think the treehouse is a perfect place to raise a baby.'

He gave her a silly side-eye. 'It's not exactly traditional. The palace might not approve.'

'Oh, they'll hate it,' she said, still smiling.

'In which case…' Oliver got out of his chair, knelt in the grass in front of her and dug into his pocket. He looked down at the small box he held in his hand then said, 'Princess Amelia of Karolinska…?'

'Yes…' she answered warily.

He dipped his eyes, then lifted his gaze so that all she could see was his gorgeous face, open and honest.

'Will you do me the honour of moving in to my not-very-royal residence once we are wed?'

Every fibre of Lia's being was caught in the brilliant flare of Oliver's smile—so much so that she barely noticed the beautiful ring he was slipping on to her finger. When she saw it, her heart melted even more. It was beautiful. An eternity ring. Something that in its colours symbolised her country, their child and, she hoped, the future they would share together. It sang of hope and promise. Joy. Something she'd never equated with marriage.

'Yes,' she said, leaning in for a kiss. 'Yes, please.'

Dinner forgotten, their kisses quickly intensified, leading them to the bedroom, where they discovered a new level of tenderness, a higher plane of ecstasy and a deeper vein of unity.

Later, as they lay in one another's arms, Lia snuggled in close to Oliver's embrace. It was amazing to think this wasn't just a one-off. It was her new reality. She was engaged to Oliver. They were going to have a child. They were going to be a family.

The only thing they had to do was make sure the palace's interference was part of their lives only up until they wed. After that she wanted things to be just as they were now.

Her phone pinged with a text.

The palace.

She threw it into the bedside table drawer. Tonight the palace could wait.

'I see your new fan is back.'

Lia's long-time surgical scrub nurse Grace— a wonderful local woman, with just about the driest sense of humour she'd ever come across—flicked her eyes up to the viewing gallery where, front and centre, Oliver sat midway through eating his lunch.

He waved and smiled. Her heart skipped a beat, then recommenced with a newer, happier cadence.

'Fiancé, you mean,' she parried, pleased that she'd managed a vaguely casual tone.

Grace's eyebrows rose.

Fair enough. They hadn't exactly been giggling together by the water cooler over her change in status. Going from a total loner to being engaged to someone she hadn't so much as mentioned deserved the odd *Are you sure about this?* look.

The truth was, she hadn't even put in her vacation form to Nate—which was a bit stupid, since the palace had changed its mind about the wedding taking place in St Victoria and now wanted it to be in Karolinska, in a 'small private ceremony' in the palace gardens.

She'd protested. Loudly.

Oliver had talked her away from the edge of the cliff by reminding her that choosing their battles would be a wise way to go in advance of her having the baby. They weren't building a track record of conceding to the palace's will... they were building an arsenal—showing willing so that when push came to shove they had ammunition.

She'd had to do the same for him when his parents had revealed their guest list. 'Some of these cousins must've been unearthed from the family mausoleum,' he'd said in disbelief.

'Ammunition,' she'd said to him, and she'd called the palace, green-lighting the Duke of Banford's invitations. 'Ammunition.

Another plus point. She didn't have to worry about planning the wedding or having it invade the lives they lived here.

After ordering some spirit-lifting chocolate

cake from the clinic's restaurant, she and Oliver had agreed that they'd fly in, pretend it was the equivalent of a Vegas-style wedding, then fly back home and do something special, just the two of them, to celebrate.

But between the baby, the wedding and the shiny new fiancé, she needed something in her life to stay the same—and that something was work.

'I hope he's not expecting you to do anything fancy today.' Grace clicked her tongue disapprovingly. 'This isn't a bells and whistles number. But it's important.'

'Of course!' Amelia replied, horrified that Grace would think she'd do anything less than her best on any of the surgeries. 'All the surgeries we do here are important.'

It was a straightforward endovascular coiling for an elderly musician's cerebral aneurysm. The minimally invasive technique meant they wouldn't need to make an incision into the skull, and if they were successful the aneurysm would be prevented from rupturing.

Grace clicked again, then continued, clearly unpersuaded, 'We need your full concentration, so I hope you don't plan on blowing him kisses—'

This wasn't like Grace. 'No! *Heavens, no. I'm scrubbed in, aren't I?*'

Her eyes flicked up to Oliver's. He winked and blew her a kiss, clearly having heard the entire thing. A delicious spray of sparkles danced around her tummy. He was so scrummy. And sweet. And kind. And she had never, ever in her life been quite so smitten, quite so quickly.

Pregnancy hormones? Or maybe it was the guy? He wasn't just a wonderful lover. He was an amazing friend. A confidant. Someone she could have an insane morning bed head with, and someone she also wanted to dress up for. He was the real deal and, rather amazingly, he was all hers.

Grace's forehead was a crease of frown lines.

A mischievous thought popped into her head. *Just to wind Grace up*, she justified, and she air-kissed her surgical glove, then blew it up to the viewing deck. Oliver caught it and pressed it to his heart, then took a big, happy bite of his sandwich.

Lia began to hum as she turned her attention to the surgical tray Grace had none too ceremoniously placed in front of her with a loud, aggrieved, sigh.

Was this what it was like to fall in love? To smile at an instrument tray, knowing the person you cared about was there to support you? She hoped so. With every cell in her body she hoped so. Because it felt great. Unlike anything she'd ever experienced.

'Your patient here is a national treasure, I'll have you know.' Grace was clearly unconvinced that Lia's focus was where it should be.

'Grace,' Lia insisted, 'I'm right here. We're going to do the very best we can.'

Grace harrumphed.

That had Lia's full attention. 'What's going on?' she asked.

Grace swished around the surgical table without saying anything, then stopped and looked Lia in the eye. 'He played at my wedding,' Grace said, a slight catch in her voice. 'That man blessed our marriage with his music and— and I don't want to play any part in seeing those magical skills destroyed.'

'Hey…' Lia soothed. 'We're a dream team. We won't let him come to any harm. I promise.'

It was the first time Lia had ever seen Grace

grow emotional over a patient. She thought of the guitarist who'd been playing when Oliver had first taken her in his arms. That music would be with her for ever, she realised, and finally she answered the question that had been playing through her mind for days.

Yes. She was falling in love.

Grace made a decidedly different noise beneath her surgical mask. The crinkles round her eyes suggested she was finally smiling. 'Girl, that man up there has definitely done something to you. Did you know that's the first time you've not gone all "instruction manual" on me?'

Lia snorted, then said, 'What does that mean?'

'Oh, you know… You're not exactly the cuddly, huggy type.'

'I've hugged you—' Lia began, then stopped herself…because maybe she hadn't.

Grace lowered her voice. 'Don't take offence, Doctor. We're used to how you are now.'

'How *am* I?'

'Clinical. You know… Like a training manual. You're all *"Hand me the fluoroscopy aids"* this and *"arterial occlusion"* that. You're… Well, you can't help the way you are. It's not everyone who goes in for emotional folderol, and you're definitely not one of 'em. But it looks like being with Dr Bainbridge up there has made you much nicer. We all like it. I just want to make sure it isn't pulling your focus away from where it should be during working hours.'

She threw a pointed glare up to the viewing room.

'I—' Lia began to protest, her cheeks pinking with the knowledge that Oliver was listening to all of this, and growing properly red when she realised Grace was right.

In her three years here, Lia had made no actual friends—least of all amongst the surgical staff with whom she spent the bulk of her time. She'd always blamed it on her upbringing, but perhaps she'd played a bigger role in her isolation than she'd thought. With that instinctive tendency to keep people at arm's length.

She was like the Princess in *Frozen*. With a warm heart chilled to the marrow because of the burden she bore through an accident of birth.

She looked up to the viewing deck again. Oliver was there, elbows on his knees, all his focus on her.

Her heart gave a hot, skippy beat. They'd had a lovely week. They'd shared meals with other doctors Oliver knew from the clinic and the hospital. Met the locals who Oliver played football with once a week. She'd even exchanged numbers with a teenager who volunteered at the hospital and was considering becoming a surgeon.

Gosh… Grace was right. Oliver Bainbridge was her very own climate change. With his resoluteness of character, his passion for his work and, more to the point, his ability to look past his own cold upbringing and become the warm, caring soul he was… The man exuded possibility. And he was changing her. For the better.

She held her hand above her heart and hoped he knew what it meant. He was melting her heart.

The surgery, happily, went like clockwork.

It was quite an interesting technique and, more importantly for her patient, a lifesaver. It involved inserting a microcatheter with a coil attached through a surgical catheter. Once she'd manoeuvred the microcatheter into the aneurysm, she sent an electrical current through, to separate the coil from the catheter, thereby sealing the opening of the aneurysm.

The patient would need to spend a night or two in the clinic, so they could monitor his progress, but she assured Grace that he would be playing his guitar again as if none of this had happened within a handful of days.'

The rest of the day passed in a blur. After her final surgery and a quick shower she wandered down to the paediatrics department, where she knew she'd find Oliver. It was his regular day at The Island Clinic, and they usually had take-away from the clinic restaurant.

He was just leaving a patient's room, and he'd spotted her, his smile brightening, when a nurse approached him with a worried expression on her face.

Oliver gave Lia a quick wave of acknowledge-ment, but listened intently as the nurse, Maddy Orakwee, told him about the call she'd just had from St Victoria Hospital.

His heart crumpled in on itself as he listened. 'Élodie? Really?'

He raked a hand through his hair, as if the gesture would alter the facts.

Maddy nodded, her expression grim.

His young patient had been released a few days ago, with multiple cautions to call if her fever returned or any of her symptoms worsened. A tough ask for a six-year-old girl who was as full of life as she was.

'She's heading for a case of secondary pneumonia,' Maddy said apologetically.

'They've given her antibiotics?'

Maddy nodded. 'They've put her on oxygen and a drip, but...' She glanced over at Lia, who wasn't doing a very good job of pretending to read a magazine nearby.

'Come on over, Lia,' he said, and then, to Maddy, 'You've met my fiancée, haven't you? Dr Trelleburg? She's the head surgeon over in the neurology department.'

Maddy nodded, and smiled at Lia.

'You were saying about Élodie?' Oliver continued.

'The nurses mentioned she was a favourite of yours, and as it's out of hours, and the emergency room is slammed...'

'Why is the ER so busy? Has there been an accident?' he asked.

Maddy had his and Lia's full attention now.

'Nothing too serious. There were a few stags—you know...' She made a 'muscle man' pose.

'Men having a stag party?' Lia asked.

'Yes. Exactly. Anyway, they were out on jet skis, showing off for a group of girls on a hen do, and—' She threw up her hands, as if that explained everything.

Oliver nodded. She didn't need to spell it out. Wedding season on the island meant one thing: a lot of alcohol-related showing off. Drink, the ocean, and motorised vehicles never made a good combination.

Oliver glanced at his watch. 'Élodie's not alone, though, right?'

'No. There are obviously staff on the ward. But...' The nurse bit the inside of her cheek.

There's no one special there just for her.

The staff at the hospital did their best to make every child feel safe and secure, offering beds in the rooms to parents and loved ones, with nurses and doctors regularly popping in to check on them, but with the hospital slammed, and no spare hands on deck, some children felt the energy of the ward shift away from them and, as such, needed an extra dose of TLC.

Élodie was one of those children. Ultrasensitive to the slightest change of focus.

'What about her aunt and uncle? Is one of them able to go in?'

Maddy's eyes darted between the pair of them, as if she were deciding to confess something, and then she blurted, 'They can't come in for the next three days. They're doing the catering on an island cruise that's not back until the end of the week.'

'What?' *Oh, hell.* 'Where was she meant to stay at night?'

Maddy shrugged. 'Another relative, maybe? I don't know. But in her condition she'll need to stay in hospital for at least the next few nights.'

Oliver stemmed a few curses on the little girl's behalf. Élodie's aunt and uncle worked hard. They each held down two and sometimes three jobs at the local resorts, trying to make ends meet. A private catering job on a yacht meant a lot of extra money.

He knew they would never have made the decision to leave her lightly. They would've put some provision in place for her care. But with their own children to look after, and jobs to complete, staying nights at the hospital was out of the question.

A fortnight ago he would have jumped in his Jeep and headed straight to the hospital. But his reality was different now. He was engaged. He was going to be a father.

He and Lia had agreed that their work wouldn't be sidelined during the lead-up to the wedding, and this week had been a particularly busy one. After a few late nights at work, they had promised each other they'd have dinner tonight. Just the two of them. So that they could regroup, look through the ream of lists the palace had sent for them to go over for the wedding and, most importantly, they write their vows.

While there had been a few lost wars in their skirmishes with the palace over flowers, venue, dresses, even the bows on the chairs, Lia had been adamant about putting their own stamp on the vows, refusing to let the palace have a final say in how they committed their lives to one another.

But Élodie… His eyes drifted to the exit.

'Bring her here,' Lia said, as if reading his

mind. 'There are free beds. We can check in on her throughout the night—if you're staying,' she said in a low voice. 'Otherwise take the helicopter back to Williamtown. It'll cut half an hour off your journey.'

'You sure?' He wasn't asking about the timing and she knew it.

'Of course.'

He sought her eyes for any sign of wavering and saw none.

Her smile softened, and she reached out to touch his arm. 'Otherwise you'll spend the entire night wanting to be where you *should* be...'

He gave her a questioning look.

'With your favourite patient,' she finished.

'I don't have favourites,' he protested. Feebly.

Both Maddy and Lia rolled their eyes. So much for being Dr Unpredictable.

He saw her gesture for what it was. Selflessness. Lia had never had anyone in her life who had put her first. He'd wanted her to know he would be the man to fulfil that role. But...

He took her hand in his. 'You're sure you're sure?'

She squeezed his hand in place of a verbal answer. It was a yes. She was sure.

Oliver felt his reality shift as he continued to wrestle with his decision. He wanted to be the man Lia could rely on—and not just because it was his duty as the father of their child, but because he was falling for her.

'We can sort out her transfer together, yeah?' Lia said, shifting into action mode. 'Then maybe get a snack later, from one of the chefs.'

He grinned. Last week's 'snack' had been a luxurious seafood platter for two. Who knew what the chefs would magic up tonight?

He tucked the happy thought of a midnight snack with Lia away, and focused on the here and now.

A mad half-hour of information-gathering ensued.

One of the 'show-offs' on the jet skis had turned out to be a famous rap star from Miami. He was best man to his producer, who was getting married at a private estate on the island. The rapper, C-Life, had been trying to pull off some wild manoeuvre, and had ended up slicing the cords on a passing kite surfer's rig, before flipping his vehicle and himself into a shallow part of the bay.

The extent of his injuries was still unknown,

but his entourage had insisted he be brought to the clinic, where his entire team could be housed in the luxurious hotel there if needed.

The helicopter pilot agreed to do a return journey to St Victoria Hospital, where Élodie was collected and brought back to The Island Clinic.

When the helicopter's arrival was announced Lia gave Oliver a kiss on the cheek, then said, 'I'm going to head over to Intake and see if there's anything I can do to help with the stag party crew. Unless you want me to stay?'

'You go on ahead. We'll catch up in a bit, okay?'

'Okay.' She grinned, her thumb playing at the edge of her engagement ring as if she'd been doing it for ever.

He could get used to this, Oliver thought as he dropped a kiss on the crown of her head before heading off to the helicopter pad. Working together. Playing together. Giving each other enough room to stay true to the person they'd both fought to become.

Lia understood that his work was a calling, more than a job, and more importantly she respected that. He'd got so used to prioritising his work, he'd have to ensure she knew she and the baby were every bit as important to him.

An hour later, after Élodie's oxygen levels had been restored to normal and a fresh antibiotic IV was in place, he gave the little girl a smile.

'Story time?' She looked at him hopefully.

'Story time,' he confirmed.

She scooched over to make room for him on her bed, her lungs making a little wheezing sound as she did so. It took all his power not to gather her up in his arms and promise her he'd look after her always.

Once he was in place, she looked up at him with expectant eyes.

There weren't any books to hand, so he'd have to make a story up tonight. 'What kind of story do you want to hear? Scary?'

She shook her head. 'No.'

'Funny?'

She gave a *Maybe* shrug, then said, 'I want a story about a princess!'

Out of the corner of his eye he caught a glimpse of Lia, in the doorway. She gave him a tiny fingertip wave, then put her index finger to her mouth, indicating that he should go ahead with his story.

'A story about a princess, eh?' he said, thinking for a moment. An interesting challenge, given he was a handful of metres from a real-life one.

'Once upon a time,' he began, 'there was a beautiful princess who lived on an island a lot like this.'

Élodie sighed and let the mountain of pillows she was propped on take her weight, tipping her head onto his arm.

Lia tipped her own head to the doorframe, ankles crossed, clearly settling in to hear the story as well.

'This particular princess,' he continued, 'had never been very good at sleeping.'

'Why?' Élodie asked with a yawn.

'Someone kept putting peas under her mattress.'

'Why would they do that?'

'To see if it made her uncomfortable.'

'Couldn't she just eat the peas?'

He laughed. 'Yes, she could. But the peas were a test.'

'What for?'

Lia's eyebrows rose.

'To find out if she was a real princess.'

'How could a pea know if she was a real princess?'

'It would be proof,' Oliver said, about to explain that it would prove how sensitive she was, because princesses had supernatural sensitivity.

But then, catching Lia's slight flinch as she defensively crossed her arms, he swerved from the original fairy tale. From everything he'd seen, Lia was made of strength, and she was the only one who didn't see it.

'The fact she could feel the pea was not only proof she was a princess—it was proof she was an *extraordinary* princess.'

'How was she extraordinary?' Élodie asked.

'She had a heart as big as the kingdom she'd promised to be loyal to. It was hard, sometimes, having a heart that big. There were days when she felt like hiding away from all those feelings, but then a stranger came into her life.'

'A handsome stranger?'

He smiled. 'Terrifically handsome. But he was also very wise. He admired the Princess for her brains as well as her beauty. And all he wanted to do was to protect her, and her beautiful heart, and all those feelings that came with it that made sleeping on peas so very difficult.'

Lia swept a tear away from her cheek.

'And the handsome Prince could tell all of that from a pea?' Élodie's eyebrows arrowed up into a confused peak.

'Oh, he wasn't a prince.'

Élodie crinkled her nose. 'What was he? A frog?'

Lia stifled a giggle, swiping at another tear.

'Sort of. He was a duke. Not as fancy as a prince, but it did mean he understood the Princess and the world she came from.'

'And he's covered in warts?' Élodie said earnestly.

'Yes. Absolutely. All over.'

'Does he love her?'

Lia uncrossed her ankles and looked away, as if seeking an immediate escape route.

'He's falling in love with her,' Oliver said, his eyes just managing to catch Lia's. 'He thinks she's amazing, and he'll do everything in his power to make sure she knows how special she is.'

Lia's hands flew to her chest. He wondered

if the same knot of emotion coiling at the base of his throat was coiling in hers.

'So will he eat the pea?' Élodie asked, clearly much more focused on the fictional Princess's discomfort.

'Yes, he will. He'll eat all the peas he has to in order to keep her happy. And he'll also go to bed once story time is over.'

After a few more minutes of wrapping up the story, and promising he'd be in first thing in the morning to see her, Oliver gave Élodie's hair a light rub and switched off her bedside light.

When he came out of the room Lia didn't say anything. She didn't have to. Her eyes were still glistening with tears as she took his hand.

'Hungry?' he asked.

She shook her head.

'Shall we go and get some sleep?'

She nodded, her grip on his hand tightening.

But when her eyes met his, lit with a passion he'd not yet seen in them, he knew that sleep was the last thing on her mind. Which suited this particular frog prince perfectly.

CHAPTER NINE

'HERE YOU GO.' Lia handed Oliver a cup of coffee, her body tingling at how pleasurable the everyday gesture was. Maybe because it wasn't everyday to her. It was all deliciously new.

'Mmm…thanks. Smells good.' Oliver gave Lia's cheek a light kiss, took a sip of the coffee, then rearranged himself in the bed.

She liked seeing him in her bed, propped up against the pillows, with the morning light shifting through the curtains when the light breeze blew them inwards. The sexual attraction they shared was still popping and fizzing between them, but there was a new dimension to the energy they shared. Trust.

The most fiercely protected piece of her heart…and Oliver had won it.

She was amazed at how much that shared moment last night with Élodie had made her feel. It had added a new level of intimacy she had never experienced. Made something click in her psyche that she'd not known she was waiting for.

Sure. They'd said they were a team. That they'd 'battle through' the palace's wedding plans together. But who wanted to battle through something that was meant to be joyous?

Once you stripped away the title and the gold monograms and the tiaras, she was just like any other woman. One who sought multiple layers of personal fulfilment. Professional pride. A family of her own. To love and be loved in return.

Her hand swept over her stomach, her thoughts organically shifting to the tiny baby growing inside her. The child she and Oliver would love and cherish, even if its inception had been unexpected and their marriage was sanctioned rather than spontaneous.

A thought occurred to her as she poured herself a cup of herbal tea. Maybe she'd needed the nudge. It wasn't as if she had family or friends she went to when she was tied up in knots, wondering which direction to take her love life. Nor did she have any examples of a healthy, happy marriage. If there hadn't been a crown to answer to, would she have done what she had when things had got too tough in Karolinska? Moved thousands of miles away?

It had been her gut response. And then she'd written a list of facts, in preparation for speaking to the palace. She'd met an amazing man and had accidentally fallen pregnant. She was going to have the baby. She didn't think he felt the same way, so she'd move and save him the trouble of rejecting her.

It was about as Princess Elsa as it got. 'Solving' the problem by removing herself from it.

Fear didn't just make for self-protective behaviour. It also made her myopic. Unable to see what was glaringly obvious. True happiness only came from finding the courage to love, even if that love came with vulnerability.

A wash of guilt churned through her. Was that what her mother had gone through? A loss of control because her father had been raised to believe whatever path he chose was the right one, to the exclusion of his wife's hopes and dreams?

'C'mon over, gorgeous.' Oliver patted the space beside him on the bed, then put on a grand voice. 'Prepare yourself for my great oratory!'

She took a seat in the small eggshell-blue armchair across from the bed. 'I'm ready.'

'What?' he said in mock despair. 'Is my morning breath too horrible to be near?'

'No.' She laughed, her conscience giving her a sharp sting as it pierced through to a deep layer of guilt.

Her 'vows notebook' was still embarrassingly blank. She hadn't been able to nail down what she wanted to say yet. How could she, when everything between them was so fresh and changeable? When she'd not yet been able to tell him she was falling in love with him?

'I've got a better view of you from here.' She gave him her most erudite look. 'Seeing as you've worked so hard on it, I want to… you know…give what you've written room to breathe.'

'That's very generous of you.' He gave her a curious look.

She tried to mimic his lofty, regal tone. 'It's how we at the royal palace like to receive and disseminate information…from a distance.'

She'd meant it humorously, but something dark flickered through Oliver's eyes. Wariness.

'Sorry.' She grimaced, pressing her hands

together into a prayer position over her heart. 'I am genuinely interested. More than interested. This is important. I'm just— I haven't written anything yet, and if what you've done is even close to what I want to say, but don't know how to...'

The muscles in Oliver's torso stretched and grew taut, as if he were bracing himself for a blow. His bare chest was distracting. It was all manly and tanned and begging for her to touch it.

She swallowed, and very possibly made a tiny whimpering noise. In a rush, she blurted, 'And if I don't sit over here I'm going to have to rip off your boxers, and you know where that leads, and then we'll both be late for work, and that would be a bad thing. The vows are important. *You're* important.'

They stared at each other. Lia's breath was coming in quick bursts, as if she'd just been running or...slightly more accurately...having athletic sex.

'It would be a very bad thing. Being naked. Together. Before work. Not listening to your vows. Right?' Her tongue swept across her lips.

The atmosphere between them sparked,

charged with that delicious shared sexual sizzle. Oliver's shoulders rolled back in a proud, leonine move that gave her a jolt of pride. *She'd* brought that on. Her desire for him had ignited his.

His eyes flicked to the clock. 'We have twenty minutes.' His blue eyes darkened. 'You can do a lot of things in twenty minutes.'

He was right. You could. If you put your mind and your body to the task at hand.

A hot, fast, and utterly sinful session of lovemaking followed. They devoured one another as if it were their first and last time together.

Screaming when she climaxed wasn't an option, because she could hear the clinic's gardeners just beyond her cottage, but the added frisson leant an even sexier edge to their utterly carnal session of hungry kisses and fingernails scraping down the length of each other's back.

A fierce, possessive entry into her most feminine essence forced Lia to stem yet more cries of pleasure by biting down on Oliver's shoulder. Hard. A move which accelerated his powerful thrusts of connection until their bodies united in climax.

As their breathing steadied, Lia ran her fingers through Oliver's hair, still sitting astride him. She revelled in the sensation of feeling both exhausted and exhilarated. Ready to take on the day, but just as excited for nightfall, when once again they would be in one another's arms.

Oliver kissed her shoulder, then shifted her so that she was snuggled up close beside him.

'There,' he said smugly. 'I knew I could get you to sit beside me.' He winked, then grabbed his notebook. 'We have seven minutes left, my beautiful bride-to-be. Now…what do you think of this?'

He put on a comically thoughtful expression, then began sonorously, 'Roses are red—'

She laughed to hide the sting of disappointment. She'd thought he was going to tell her that he loved her the way she loved him.

She supposed she couldn't blame him for his jokey tone. She didn't know how to put what she felt for *him* into words. *I love you* didn't seem a big enough statement to encapsulate everything he'd come to mean to her in such a short period of time. And *You stopped me running for the hills* wasn't exactly the most romantic thing in the world, was it?

'I think it's a very promising start,' she said finally.

He scrubbed his hand through his hair, then turned the paper. It was blank.

Oh. He really hadn't written anything.

He lifted up the printout of suggestions the palace had sent. 'These all seem a little bit dry.'

'As the Sahara!' she agreed, so as not to betray her genuine hurt.

But her response had clearly lurched into the 'too emphatic a response' territory, because Oliver's expression turned serious.

He tucked a finger under her chin and gave her a feather-soft kiss. 'Hey… We'll nail these vows. We'll write something that's personal to us and easily approved by the palace.' He dipped his head so he could catch her eye. 'Trust me?'

She wanted to. More than anything, she wanted to. That was what truly loving him would mean. Trusting him with all her heart.

She sought his eyes for one solitary sign that what they were doing was a bad idea and couldn't find one. Perhaps the pregnancy hormones were also making her paranoid.

A swelling of hope and wistfulness filled her

chest as he pulled her close, his warm, citrussy scent surrounding her. 'I wish we were getting married like normal people,' she said.

'We're normal people,' Oliver insisted.

'Not really.' She snuggled in under the comforting weight of his arm. 'I mean…it's not like the gardens in the palace are awful, or anything, but…there's no spontaneity. Not when we have to do everything with a spotlight on us.'

'Like what?'

She shrugged and said the first thing that came to mind. 'What if you want to have a stag do?'

He snorted. 'Get drunk and ride jet skis? No, thank you.'

'I'm pretty sure that's not the only thing men do on their stags. Go on. World's your oyster. What would you do?'

She pulled the sheet around her a bit and twisted her hips so that they were facing one another.

He thought for a moment. 'You know, this probably won't sound very macho, but I'd love to bring some of the kids from the local orphanage down to Turtle Cove to go snorkelling. Have a blow-out picnic. Maybe get some of the other doctors to come down and play some footie. Bring Élodie along. You know…'

She finished his sentence for him. 'Act like the fathers they'll never have?'

The tiny crinkles alongside his eyes deepened as he checked an emotional breath. 'Yeah…'

'Like the father *you* never had?' she guessed.

The crinkles deepened again. This time he just nodded.

Her heart squeezed tight and she silently admonished herself for ever doubting him. So what if he hadn't written his vows? He'd had the same emotionally strangled upbringing she had. One in which you simply didn't express how you felt as it would more often than not be dismissed as 'inappropriate'.

She laced her fingers through his and sat back against the headboard with a sigh. 'I don't have a clue what I'd do if I were having a hen do.'

'No?' His smile was soft and sincere.

'I probably wouldn't have one.' She gave a weak smile. 'Atleast it would please the King and Queen.'

'Go on…' Oliver gave her a nudge. 'What would you like for your fantasy hen do? Tutus?

Pin the tail on the paediatrician? Sky's the limit!'

She laughed, flushed a bit, then sheepishly admitted, 'I'd want the equivalent of a twelve-year-old's birthday party.'

He hooted, then clapped his hands, looking both delighted and bewildered. 'What? Why? Didn't you have one?'

'Yes, but it involved more of this…' she did a regal wave '…than this.' She waved her hands in the air as if she were wielding a pair of pom-poms. She glanced at the clock. 'Crikey. We've got to get hopping. I've got surgery soon.'

'Tell me?' he asked, pulling her up out of bed and towards the shower. 'Tell me exactly what twelve-year-old Amelia would have done for her birthday if she'd been in charge?'

And somehow, over the course of him soaping her naked body and helping her dry off, and eventually managing to get each other into their scrubs for a day at the clinic, she did.

Lia finished extracting the surgical camera from the viewing tube. 'Right. Looks like we can close.'

'Hand it over, honey. I don't want you dropping that thing in your excitement.' Grace's quiet cackle made it clear she was teasing.

Lia hadn't seen Oliver for a few days, and even their dinner date today had been provisional. Tourist season had a way of being crazy season in the clinic and the hospital, and this summer was no different.

Grace held out her hand as Lia just stood there. She knew she looked like a numpty, grinning behind her mask at her lovely fiancé. Even so, she couldn't help a slightly miffed, 'I'd never compromise a patient's safety.'

'I know. I'm just saying…'

Grace made one of her *I see everything* noises which, over the three weeks since she'd first met Oliver, had shifted from protective and judgmental to quietly approving. Oliver had noticed the shift too, and had lately taken to bringing Grace small boxes of her favourite coconut sweets, which were only available in Williamstown.

Lia handed over the camera, her smile still hidden behind her surgical mask. To be honest, it had been nice having Grace go all 'Mama Bear' around her. It was the closest she'd come to having a friendship in years. The closest she'd come to experiencing a mother's protectiveness.

'Thank you, Grace,' she said, and then, to the team, 'Another job well done.'

Lia asked her number two to close the small incision they'd needed for the operation and kept her walk as casual and relaxed as she could until she hit the changing rooms, when her pace quadrupled. After a quick shower, she was towelling herself off when Grace came in.

'Lover boy's outside.'

She grinned. 'We're having dinner.'

'I thought you were going to Florida.'

'Oh, *crumbs*!' Her heart sank. 'I completely forgot.'

She had a consultation with a prospective patient who refused to travel to St Victoria without a meeting on her 'home turf' first. She was a grand dame of the Orlando resort scene, if the rumour mill was anything to go by. One with a brain tumour that other doctors had deemed impossible to remove.

Her shoulders drooped. 'Got any good *Whoops, I messed up* lines?'

Grace raised her eyebrows and gave her a mysterious look. 'I'm sure you'll figure something out.'

When Lia came out of the locker room she was surprised to see Oliver with an overnight bag slung over his shoulder and one of her wheelie bags by his foot.

'What's going on?'

'Don't you worry, Your Highness. All your dreams will come true where we're heading.'

She winced. 'Oliver, I can't. I'm going to see a patient.'

'That you are.' He tapped the side of his nose and, with a wink, added, 'And you're going to be escorted to the wilds of Florida by yours truly.'

It was a nice turn of events, but… 'Don't you have work?

'Not for the next forty-eight hours.'

From inside the dressing room she could hear Grace singing. Also unusual… What was going on? 'Oliver. This is weird. Nice weird, but…' Her eyebrows drew together. 'Why are you coming to Florida with me?'

His smile broadened. 'You'll see.'

* * *

'You want me to *what*, now?' Lia threw Oliver an uncertain look as they approached the clinic's private airport.

She held up the wig he'd just handed her, as if she'd just had an *Aha!* moment. The hair was as dark and curly as hers was blonde and straight.

'This isn't some untapped sexual fantasy you want fulfilled before you marry a blonde Scandinavian girl, is it?' She gave her hips a rather too alluring swish.

'No!' Oliver waved his hands in protest. He was seeking discretion, not indiscretion. Although now that she mentioned it…

No.

Playing naughty dress-up was not the point of this trip.

'Oliver? What's going on?' She glanced nervously over her shoulder. 'I don't want the clinic thinking I'm compromising a patient meeting with…you know…our sexy-sexy business.'

He tried and failed to ignore the tug of response. He liked it that they had sexy-sexy business. But she looked worried. Maybe he should just tell her.

No.

The wheels were already in motion, her boss knew exactly what was happening, and now was as good a time as any for her to find out that he was a man who loved setting up surprises. The good kind. It was a big part of who he was, so she might as well know what she was marrying into before he slid the ring on her finger.

An unwelcome chill slipped through him as he thought of his parents' enormous, unwelcoming estate. The one they were still expecting him to move in to once he was married. That would be a surprise, too. One he still hadn't figured out how to handle.

Ignoring the discomfort that came from holding something that important back from her, he held up another wig and popped it on his own head. 'We're both going in disguise.'

'Why? This is a legal flight.' Her expression turned horrified. 'Someone didn't alert the press, did they?'

'No. Absolutely not.' He'd made sure of that.

She scrunched up her face in confusion. 'I'm happy you're coming, but…wigs? I don't understand. This is a simple business trip, Oli.'

'There's someone the hospital's paediatrics

team want me to check up on,' he answered smoothly. Too smoothly.

Lia didn't miss it. 'There's something else.' She narrowed her gaze. 'What's going on, Oliver Bainbridge?'

He gave her a mischievous grin, 'You'll find out soon enough.'

'And I need to wear this?' She pulled on the wig, without bothering to tuck her blonde hair beneath the bonnet of dark curls.

He laughed and pulled her to him for a kiss, enjoying the fact that she leaned into him as his lips met hers. It was a sign she was falling for him as much as he was falling for her.

So why not tell her about the UK estate? Tell her how much having this baby with her meant to him? Or, more to the point, why not tell her he loved her?

A knot of discomfort needled at his conscience.

It was a difficult truth to acknowledge but, as much as he cared for Lia, and as happy as he was knowing their future would be a shared one, he was still protecting the part of his heart that had been hurt when his ex had made her decision about her pregnancy.

He was going to have to find a way to lay that to rest. And soon.

Lia looked up at him, sensing his tension. 'Oli?'

Her eyes had gone a deeper shade of blue. Dark with concern. With affection. And very possibly with love. The same slightly guarded love he felt for her. It was a hurdle they simply had to get over before exchanging those vows with one another.

He couldn't marry her with secrets held close to the same heart that beat for her and their child. He'd tell her. About everything. But for now, he hoped the grand gesture she was about to experience would tell her just how much he cared.

He smiled, kissed his index finger, then popped it on her nose. 'All in good time, my darling bride-to-be. All in good time.'

The journey to Orlando was uneventful, if he didn't count Lia playing twenty questions with him for the entire flight.

Luckily, he'd had practice in keeping secrets. He'd given presents to the children at his boarding school whose parents had been too busy to fly them home for the holidays. To draw out the fun, he would hide the gifts and play the whole thing out a bit like an Easter egg hunt.

If his parents hadn't demanded his presence for the annual holiday family photos, he would've happily stayed at school and played board games or read books to the younger children, because leaving those little sad faces behind had seemed ridiculous when he had known the last thing he'd be receiving at home was a warm welcome. He'd made the best of his childhood...but sometimes it had been tough finding the silver linings.

'Hey.' Lia tapped him on the knee as they rode in a limousine to the resort hotel. 'You okay?'

He swept her hand to his lips and gave the back of it a kiss. 'Absolutely. Just taking a little trip down memory lane.'

'Not a very nice one from the looks of it.' She frowned.

He dropped a soft kiss on her cheek, then tipped his forehead to hers. 'Not to worry. All the memories will be good from now on.'

She moved his hand to her stomach. 'We're

going to give this one nothing but happy memories, right?'

There was an urgency in her question that he felt in his marrow.

It was their shared fear. That the childhoods they'd had—mired in tradition rather than love—would become their own child's future… for better or for worse. Which was exactly why he'd been struggling with writing his wedding vows to Lia. He wanted them to show her that he had worked so hard to change…to be different. That he wanted more than anything to take a spear to his heart for her. Fight for her.

The easiest way to communicate that was very simple. Three little words that meant the world. Three little words he had yet to say to Lia.

'Hey.' He gave her thigh a rub. 'Did you get your vows written?'

She crinkled her nose. 'Sorry. Still working on them.'

He gave his watch a dramatic tap. 'Only ten more days!'

'Ugh.' Lia dropped her head into her hands. 'Don't remind me!'

'Hey.' He cupped her cheeks in his hands and turned her face so that he could look into her eyes. If she was having second thoughts about anything, she needed to let him know. 'If you don't want to do this—'

'No.' She put up her hands. 'I mean, yes. I do want to do it. With all my heart. I—'

She stopped herself, and by the way her cheeks coloured Oliver was sure she'd been about to tell him she loved him. He hoped that was true. With every fibre in his being.

He was prepared to sacrifice so much for her and their child. His anonymity. His desire to step away from his 'birthright' duties. His quiet life which, once they were wed, he knew wouldn't be quiet any more. But all that sacrifice would be for a much greater joy. Having a family of his own. To love and to cherish. To honour and protect. He would do all those things and more, but he had to know they were a team.

Which made the fact he wanted to hear it from her a case of the pot calling the kettle black.

'What is it that scares you the most?' he asked her.

She bit down on her lip, then admitted, 'That you'll walk away.'

The confession gripped his heart and then squeezed one painful beat after another out of it until he found his voice again and assured her, 'That will never happen.'

Deep down, he knew he did love her. That he did have the strength to confront his parents… make changes. To trust in Lia the way she was trying to trust in him. He just needed it all to rise through his past, heal it and surface.

She gazed into his eyes for a moment longer and must have found the answer she was looking for, because she leant into a kiss that accepted the spoken and the silent promises.

They could do this, he told himself as the driver announced they were at their destination. They could give themselves, and their child, the happiest of lives.

'Pretty luxurious,' Oliver said as they entered the hotel's penthouse suite.

Lia agreed. 'I don't know what this patient does for a living, but she clearly does well if she can put us up here.'

Together they scanned the place in disbelief. It was even better than he'd imagined when he'd booked it. He presumed Lia was used to luxurious hotel rooms, and he was certainly no stranger to them, but this was on another level.

Floor-to-ceiling windows. Glass. Chrome. A huge rooftop garden with an infinity pool and a waterfall. Towering fruit baskets. A butler who offered a pet hire service in case they were missing their animals from home. A private chef who was on hand to make fresh sushi.

They could have anything they desired— apart from a swim at the lake, which apparently had an alligator in it, but the staff were seeing about offering the gator 'relocation services'.

Lia shot Oliver an embarrassed look. 'Er... I hope you don't get used to this. My princess allowance won't really go this far for our family holidays.'

Oliver laughed and shook his head, as if to say a solid *Don't you worry.* 'I'd be happy with a picnic down at the beach. This is much more my parents' kind of thing than mine.'

As well as the 'old money' his father had inherited, his father's work as a property mogul meant his parents were amongst the wealthiest couples in England. Something they rarely let him forget whenever they tried to pin down his plans for the family fortune once they were gone.

He was happy with his treehouse and a life below the radar, thank you very much. Although a couple of nights splashing out for his future wife in a place like this wasn't strictly a hardship.

He hoped she wouldn't be too cross when she found out there wasn't really a patient.

The phone in the suite rang and the butler answered it, speaking in a low murmur. When he'd finished, he approached Lia. 'Your Highness—'

'Oh, please, no,' she corrected. 'Amelia or Dr Trelleburg will be fine.'

'Dr Trelleburg,' he began again, with a deferential bow. 'That was your hostess. She says you will have to forgive her, but she isn't up to seeing you today and could she please delay your meeting until tomorrow morning?'

Oliver hid his smile as Lia gave him a confused look then said to the butler, 'Please let her know I'm happy to see her whenever it suits.'

He finished the call and turned to leave.

Lia stopped him and gave him a conspiratorial smile. 'Any chance you could let me know who it is?'

The butler stiffened. 'I'm afraid I am not privileged to know that information.'

'Oh. Okay, well...' She gave Oliver a bewildered shrug. 'I guess that means we can have that dinner date after all.' She glanced at the retreating figure of the butler. 'But do you mind if I go over the case notes for twenty minutes or so?'

'Absolutely.'

Oliver knew it was only a matter of time before she figured out that the case notes were from a surgery her mentor had done a year or so back on a cabinet member from the Costa Rican government but he needed to make a couple of quick calls.

After he'd finished, he found Lia thoughtfully eating a peach out in the rooftop garden. He gave her a kiss, enjoying the taste of her lips mingled with peach juice. She pulled back and gave a huge yawn.

'I'm so sorry. It's not you, I promise.'

He gave her hair a stroke and properly looked at her. She looked tired. Full-time work, wedding plans and being newly pregnant were obviously taking their toll. They had also spent quite a few late nights getting to know one another on a more intimate level.

'What do you think about room service and a movie in bed?' he suggested.

She clasped her hands to her chest, practically melting with pleasure at the thought. 'I would love that.'

Within about ten minutes Lia was curled up in bed, her arm wrapped round Oliver's waist as if he was her security blanket and fast asleep. Not quite the night he'd imagined, but every bit as perfect.

The next morning Lia pronounced herself well rested and full of beans.

Just as she was about to start putting on her business suit he asked, 'How do you fancy a little adventure?'

She smiled. 'I'd love to, but I've got to meet my patient.'

His expression turned into one that made it pretty clear there was no patient.

The penny dropped. 'Oliver Bainbridge… what have you done?'

'Nothing bad. Nate knows, so you're all good on the work front.'

'What did you tell him, exactly?'

'That I wanted to surprise my bride-to-be.'

'Will it require the wigs?' She held up the dark wig with a finger.

'Yes.'

One short helicopter ride later, and Amelia let out a scream of disbelief.

'Disney World?' She gave a double-take, and felt her smile reaching from ear to ear. 'I've never been to a theme park!'

Oliver had clearly been panicking that she wouldn't enjoy his surprise, and the look on his face turned to one of relief. He waved his hands. 'Happy Hen Do!'

Tears of joy sprang to Lia's eyes. He'd organised all this for her? Never once in her life had she had a surprise anything, let alone a surprise hen do.

She swept the tears away before they could fall, giggling and hiccoughing, not knowing which way to look. 'How did you know I've always wanted to come here?'

'I didn't.' Oliver was laughing, too. He handed her a tissue, using his thumb to edge away a couple of escapee tears from her cheek. 'I just thought, if I was a twelve-year-old girl…what would I want to do for my birthday? I asked the internet, and then I asked a six-year-old, and between all three of us we came up with this.'

'Élodie?' she asked, instantly thinking of the lovely bond he shared with his recently discharged patient.

'That's the one,' he said.

She wrapped her arms around him and gave him a huge, happy, sloppy kiss. She pulled back, her smile disappearing as she did. 'Hen dos are supposed to be with friends. I don't really have any.'

'Well…you've got me,' Oliver said. 'And a couple of extra people who'd like to think of you as their friend.'

He pointed towards the VIP entrance, where they were headed, and there, holding hands, were Grace and Élodie. They waved enthusiastically. Élodie was already wearing the trademark ears. Grace was too, which instantly made Lia roar with laughter.

'This is great!'

She clapped her hands, finally connecting all the dots.

'And we've got the wigs in case you want to go incognito,' he said.

'I don't want to hide away from the world. You and I are going to be a family. So let's start the way we want to continue.'

It was as close to a declaration of love as she'd let herself come. Her heart was absolutely soaring. Maybe today would be the day she threw caution to the wind and told him she loved him.

He lifted up his wig and gave her a questioning look. Her heart plummeted. Had she misread things so badly? 'Or would you rather people not know we were together?'

'No! God, no. The opposite. I'd shout it from the…' his eyes scanned the area '…the top of that palace if you wanted me to. I just want you to be comfortable. Happy.'

This was love. It had to be. They often communicated things without saying them, and this felt like one of those moments. Perfect synchronicity of their hearts and minds. Love.

'I am happy. Ridiculously happy.' She tucked her hand in the crook of his elbow. 'Thank you. This'll be the best hen party ever.'

'Well, then… It's not your kingdom, but shall

we see what sort of magic we can whip up in this one?'

He held out a hand as two 'living' cartoon characters appeared and rolled out an actual red carpet, whilst 'Cinderella' handed out tiaras to all the women and a toy sword to Oliver.

Again, Lia's smile stretched from ear to ear. 'Wild horses couldn't stop me!'

CHAPTER TEN

'THAT WAS THE BEST!'

'The fastest one, for sure! I wish you could've gone on it, Lia.'

Lia smiled. She did, too, but Oliver had gently suggested that being whipped around on a rollercoaster probably wasn't the best of things for a pregnant woman to do. He was right, of course. She must've left her common sense at the gates when she'd entered the theme park!

'I thought the one in the dark was the fastest,' Élodie assured her. It was one they'd all gone on together.

'And the scariest.' Grace shook her head. 'I'm pretty sure when I take these ears off there'll be more grey in my hair than there was at the beginning.'

'What did you think of the Peter Pan ride?' Oliver asked. 'It felt like we were flying along with them.'

'It did, didn't it? I wonder if Tinker Bell ever gets tired.'

Élodie, Grace and Oliver's banter continued unabated as they headed to the next ride while Lia just beamed. A few hours earlier she wouldn't have believed having this much fun was possible. But being with Oliver was like having a special key to entire realms of happiness she'd never imagined, let alone experienced.

She'd put on the wig, in the end. More because Élodie wanted to wear a mermaid wig and Grace was wearing her Minnie Mouse ears and a tiara, whilst Oliver was wearing a pirate hat, with a plastic sword stuffed in his belt. Rather than be the odd one out, she topped the curly mass of dark curls with a bright red baseball cap with rainbow 'ears'. Not her best look, but it was fun.

And that was what life with Oliver seemed to be all about. Maxing out the good times whilst respectfully acknowledging the tougher ones.

He was simply the best person she'd ever met in her life. Literally swoonworthy. And she was going to marry him in a few days' time. For once, she had the palace to thank for their controlling ways.

He'd chosen her 'hen party' guests perfectly as well. Huge groups weren't really her thing, so this quartet was perfect. None of the eclectic foursome had ever been to this theme park and, as such, they were all equally thrilled with the singing and dancing 'bears', the swirling teacups and even the 'abandoned' treehouse—which, unsurprisingly, Oliver had made them climb up and around twice, as he tried to figure out whether or not he could make a waterwheel out of coconuts for his own tree home.

They had all roared with laughter when Grace, normally so controlled and dignified, had laughed and screamed the loudest when they'd taken a watery rollercoaster ride on huge 'logs'. But it was Élodie who had taken the lead now they'd entered the part of the park which was almost literally awash with princesses. Rather than pity them, as was Lia's gut instinct, Élodie adored them with a passion that was utterly infectious.

'She's in her element, isn't she?' Lia asked Oliver in a low voice, as Grace queued with

Élodie to have their photograph taken with a mermaid princess.

'Princess stories are her favourites,' Oliver confirmed.

'Any particular one?' Lia asked.

'I'd love to say it's *The Princess and the Pea*, which is my favourite.' He grinned and slipped his arm round her waist, pulling her in for a light hug. 'But this week she's all about Belle.'

He shook his head and smiled, as if he were going over all the other stories they'd read together and loving it every bit as much as he had the first time round.

More love than she'd thought possible bloomed within her. This was the man who was going to love her child. Love her. If life felt this great now, who knew how happy she could be in a few years' time?

Happier than her parents were, she thought, discreetly crossing her fingers and shooting a *please* look up to the heavens.

'Belle's a big reader,' Oliver said, as if he'd given the matter serious consideration. 'Which is a good thing.' He turned his attention back to her and asked, 'What do *you* think of Belle?

A good role model for little girls? Or too much of a dreamer?'

The sting of pain that always came from re-visiting her childhood was tamped down by the realisation that Oliver genuinely cared about what sort of role models Élodie chose. Her heart practically swelled to bursting as she thought of him showing the same level of detailed concern for their own child.

She hadn't really read fairy tales when she was growing up. Nor had anyone read them to her. Her parents had made a stab at it, sure, but… They'd been busy with their failing marriage, and her nannies had been much more focused on the palace's long list of rules and restrictions rather than on the actual child they were meant to be caring for.

For her, being raised royal had been basically like being raised in another century. And not a particularly fun one.

'I have to make a confession.' Lia bit her lip and looked up into Oliver's dark blue eyes.

His brow furrowed. 'About…?'

'I'm a bit of a novice when it comes to fairy tale princesses. Which one is Belle?'

'Belle! You know… *Beauty and the Beast.*

Aaargh!' He distorted his face and turned his hands into claws, making Lia laugh.

'Which one are you, then?' she asked playfully.

'I thought it would be obvious that you, my dear, are Beauty.'

He popped a kiss on her cheek, then returned his gaze to Élodie as he briefly explained the storyline.

His smile turned thoughtful when he said, 'I think she loves Belle because she isn't scared of the Beast. She's had to face a lot of medical monsters in her time. And, of course, the loss of her parents. She's endured a lot of loss. Too much for a little girl with so much joy to share.'

He gave Lia's hand a squeeze.

'Belle's like you, as well. Smart. Thoughtful. Excellent taste in fiancés,' he added with a cheeky grin, and then, more gently, 'Maybe that's why Élodie enjoys your company so much. You've both borne too heavy a burden of loss, too young, but you're proof that all those hurdles don't have to trip you up. They make you stronger.'

Lia was about to launch into an explanation of how she had been born into her title, whereas

Belle had proactively chosen to be a princess, when what Oliver had said gained purchase.

He saw her as strong. As resilient. Someone who had overcome the struggles in her past rather than someone who had been beaten by them. She'd never looked at herself that way.

She nestled into Oliver's hug, hoping he understood how much his opinion mattered to her. How grateful she was for his positive outlook on life. He was no beast. He was a knight in shining armour. *Her* knight. And she knew in that instant that all her fears that he would change when they were married were unfounded. This was who he was. This was the man she would have the privilege of loving for the rest of her life.

They stood together, looking like all the other happy couples, enjoying the hubbub around them and, of course, Élodie's huge, beaming smile every time she turned round and waved at them, moving closer to the mermaid princess.

Oliver laughed and beamed back, waving like a proud father each time. Kindness radiated from him. His affection for the little girl went beyond that of a doctor and patient, and it dawned on her that he loved her as if she was his own.

Rather than that fact making her feel fearful, or excluded, Lia felt as if she'd been invited into a big love bubble—one that had the capacity to grow into something bigger and better the more their own family grew.

The revelation warmed Lia's heart in a way she'd never experienced. She'd been taught that love was an exclusive thing. A private thing. But it was quite the opposite. Being generous with his love didn't detract from Oliver's love for her, or the child they were going to have. It made it more powerful.

Love, she realised, was Oliver's superpower.

She wanted to give their child that same gift.

She looked at Oliver, enjoying the delight in his features when Élodie made the mermaid princess laugh when as two of them hugged while Grace took their photo. The mermaid wiggled. Élodie wiggled. The rest of the little girls in the queue wiggled. They were all giggling as if this was the very best moment in their lives.

Oliver started wiggling too, and gave her a hip-bump to make her join in.

An ache to be so fun and free wrapped around her heart and squeezed tight. Instinct, or rather training, dictated that princesses did not wiggle.

And then it hit her. Why on earth not? It clearly brought happiness and laughter, neither of which were bad things.

As if the scales had literally dropped from her eyes, Lia saw her future with a new clarity. The way she approached being a princess was up to her. It didn't have to be a horrid duty—a burden she had no choice in bearing…something that came with rules and regulations that strangled like the tightest of corsets. These princesses were all smiles and fun. Okay, sure… They were pretend princesses and they were being paid to smile… But the *joy* they were giving all these children genuinely seemed to be a *shared* joy. Something she definitely wanted to be a part of.

As they made their way around the rest of the magical kingdom Lia had Grace tell her as many princess stories as she could. Snow White's stepmother had sent her into the woods to be killed. Sleeping Beauty had been cursed by an evil fairy. Cinderella had been forced into life as a scullery maid by her stepmother.

Rapunzel's mother had given her to a witch as penance for stealing some delicious salad greens she'd craved whilst pregnant.

A few stories in, and Lia was beginning to think she'd not had it quite so bad after all.

When they arrived at the queue for Prince Charming's carousel and Grace paused for breath, Lia asked Élodie, 'Don't any of these stories frighten you?'

Élodie dramatically shook her head, as if the idea was absurd. 'Nope!'

'Why not?' Lia asked, truly interested.

'Because all the princesses win against the scary things, and the evil people usually shrivel up or disappear in a puff of smoke once they realise good is better than bad.'

'I thought the handsome princes fixed everything,' Grace said, giving Oliver an uncharacteristic wink.

Élodie pursed her lips, as if the idea were ridiculous. 'It's the *princesses* who win. They have the brains and the power. They just need to see things from a different angle and when they do...' She made a swirling motion with the magic wand Oliver had bought her. 'Everything's good again.'

'Girl power. I like it.' Lia grinned. 'Shame about the handsome princes.' She gave Oliver a good-natured elbow in the ribs. 'It's always nice to have a helping hand when the world is coming to an end.'

Élodie looked at her, still as serious as if she were working out a long division problem. 'The princesses and maidens in distress could've totally believed what the evil stepmothers and bad fairies and everyone told them—but they didn't.' She tapped her heart. 'They listened to *this*!'

She leant in to Lia and cupped her hand, as if she wanted to keep a secret from Oliver, but spoke loud enough so that they could all hear.

'A lot of people think the handsome princes do it all, but even though they're really nice, and know a lot about medicine, they are usually cuter than they are smart.'

Oliver clutched his hands to his heart. '*Oof!* What a blow to my ego! And here I was thinking I was going to save you all from peril by the end of the day.'

'Well,' Élodie conceded, 'some of the princes have nice horses, and usually a castle, and sometimes a dog. I think every princess would like a dog with fluffy ears, wouldn't she?'

Oliver choked back a laugh and gave Élodie a *good point* nod.

'Next riders on their mounts!' called the woman in charge of boarding people onto the carousel.

'You've got a great way of looking at the world,' Grace said, guiding Élodie onto a carousel horse while Lia and Oliver mounted the horses just behind them.

Lia grabbed the reins of her horse and pretended to spur it into a gallop as the carousel began its slow whir into action. 'Race you to the finish line!' she challenged Oliver, who immediately 'spurred' his own horse into a gallop.

She felt unbelievably happy. This trip to the theme park was meant to be fun, and it was, but she hadn't expected to learn an important lesson to boot. She was the mistress of her own destiny.

It was all about perspective. If she could tap into the truest part of her heart and realign her perspective…then the rest of her life would pan out to be the happiest.

A few hours later, after they'd dropped Grace

and a sleeping Élodie off at their hotel room, they climbed into bed in their sumptuous suite.

'That was the best day.'

'The best?' Oliver let out a low whistle, then pulled her to him. 'I wonder if there's any way we could make it better?'

The atmosphere between them instantly shifted from playful to sensual. As Oliver's bare skin connected with her own, Lia felt electricity pulse through her in a decidedly womanly way. Gone was the little girl princess having innocent fun. In her place was the woman, who was more than happy to show her handsome prince just how much she loved him. So she did.

In the morning, after they'd had some coffee in bed, luxuriating in the rare occurrence of having nothing to do, Lia gave in to a whim and jumped up on the bed and began to bounce. Her hair was flying every which way. She was wearing mismatched pyjamas. There was music playing. It was *fun*! The type of fun she'd never, ever been allowed to have nor, later in life, let herself have.

'What are you doing, you madwoman?' Oliver laughed.

'Things I never did as a kid.' She grinned,

beckoning for him to join her. 'It's your fault,' she said. 'You taught me that it was important to be me!'

She bounced until she was high enough to whip herself into a somersault—only to land on her back with an ungainly *thunk*.

She curled into a protective ball. 'Ow!'

Oliver's blood ran cold.

The baby.

He raced to her, all his pent-up fears about losing the chance to become a father surging through him.

'Don't move. Did you hurt your stomach? Anything else? Tell me everything.'

She gave a little groan and pushed herself up. 'I'm fine. Embarrassed at my lack of grace, but fine.' She moved her head around as proof that her neck was all right, too. She swept her hand along her stomach. 'We're both fine.'

Relief was engulfed by something else as he felt the past consume him.

'What were you thinking?' he demanded.

Lia took his face in her hands. 'Hey. I'm okay. It's okay.'

He shook her hands away and bit out in a tone

that sounded foreign even to him, 'You've got to be more careful. Don't you *want* our child?'

'Hey!' She held up her hands for him to stop—which, mercifully, he did.

They both stared at one another. Hard. Like boxers squaring off with one another before the referee rang the starting bell.

This was a side of Oliver Lia had seen tiny glimpses of, but before his concern had always felt protective, a buffer against the rest of the world, not another set of rules and regulations.

Yes, she'd made a bad decision. But enough to warrant accusing her of not wanting her child...? That was a line he shouldn't have crossed.

She reminded herself that this month had been one of extremes. That they were strangers compelled to marry because of an accidental pregnancy and the demands of the palace. Both of them had had to deal with childhoods that hadn't been the happiest. Both of them were facing a future that was very different from whatever either of them had dreamed. But she'd thought they'd found happiness in a new dream. Hadn't they?

Clinging to what remained of her calm she asked, 'Oliver? Is there something going on?'

Everything about him bore an air of gravity and stillness that instantly crushed what remained of her self-confidence. A sharp, icy sensation pierced through to her heart when he said, 'I probably should've told you this back when you found out you were pregnant...'

This was a crossroads and they both knew it. Oliver swept a hand through his hair, wishing he could pull the perfect words out of his brain.

He hadn't meant to keep this from Lia, but the longer he'd kept it to himself, the more it had gained power over him. No matter how many times he'd reminded himself that this wasn't the past, and Lia wasn't his ex, the fear that he might lose this chance at fatherhood had gnawed at his ability to truly open his heart to her.

He tried to force some rational thoughts to the fore.

Lia was her own person. A deeply proud, intelligent, controlled and very private woman who, in the handful of time they'd spent together, he'd seen blossom into a free spirit.

And, even though he hated himself for it, there was a part of him that feared the choices she might make without him.

But he loved her, and knew with every second that ticked past that he was pushing her away. She deserved to know where all this was coming from.

'I had a girlfriend once...' he began, his voice ragged with emotion.

Lia nodded for him to continue, but she pulled away from his touch, tucking her knees under her chin and wrapping her arms around them, as if cocooning herself from any harm.

'We met during our internships at Oxford.'

Again, Lia nodded, the wariness in her eyes turning the irises an almost transparent blue.

He forced the words out as neutrally as he could. 'She fell pregnant, but kept the news to herself. And then...then she "sorted it" without even discussing it with me.'

Lia frowned. 'What do you mean, she—?' She stopped herself, her expression making it clear she understood that his girlfriend had terminated the pregnancy. 'I'm so sorry, Oliver. I'm sure she had her reasons, but still... I can't imagine how that would've felt.' She reached out to him, then abruptly pulled back. 'Why would my jumping around remind you of that?'

He was going to have to choose his words carefully. They'd both grown up in strict households with an exacting list of expectations. A regime that hadn't suited either of them. This wasn't an attempt to lay down more rules. But he knew that asking her to be more cautious could come across that way.

He wanted her to know he was here for her. That he wanted to be involved. That he wanted to be a part of this journey with her, every step of the way, supporting her and their child. So when he'd seen her whirl around, then land with a thump, sprawled out on the bed, not moving, his worst fears had taken over.

'I was worried you'd hurt yourself. And the baby.'

Her frown deepened. 'Oliver, women have been doing all sorts of things whilst pregnant—including dancing and working and probably even having pillow fights—and still having healthy, happy babies. It's early days, yet. I'm not even showing. We're still within the three months when most people don't tell anyone.'

'Yes. And the reason they don't tell anyone

is because the chances of losing the baby are higher.'

She pressed her lips together, their dusty rose colour whitening from the pressure.

He didn't blame her for being angry. One doctor informing another how the body worked was ultra-patronising. Especially when that doctor was the father of your child.

Lia stared at him. Hard. 'Oliver. You brought me to an amusement park. We were riding on *rollercoasters* yesterday!'

'Yes—and I made sure you didn't go on anything that would harm the baby.'

Lia's blue eyes blazed with indignation. 'Oh, you did, did you? You kept a special eye out for me because you've decided I don't have the maternal instinct to do so myself? I'm not your ex, Oliver. I want this baby every bit as much as you do. I guess the real question I should be asking myself is, do I want you as much as I want the child?'

Oliver felt the impact of her words as if they were a physical blow. What a moment to realise he'd let his past darken his future. He loved her. He did. He wanted to build on the foundation of what they'd been sharing over these last few weeks. But something caught the words in his throat and stemmed them.

Lia swept away angry tears. 'It's pretty clear your priority is our child and not me. Which is a step up from my father's parenting skills, anyway. It's a good trick, though, Oliver. Playing the doting fiancé right up until you get your heir. Well done for keeping me wrapped up in a little princess cocoon. Bewitching me into thinking it was me you cared about.'

He wanted to pound his head against the wall. Turn back time. Anything to fix this.

Tell her you love her.

'Lia, you know I'm not like that.'

'Do I?' she asked, obviously unsatisfied with his response. 'Do I really know anything about you? Up until a few minutes ago I was pretty sure I knew you, and how you felt about me, but now... Now, I'm not so sure.'

Oliver tried to force his brain and his heart to work in tandem. Words clogged up his throat. None of them were the right ones to express how he felt. And his silence fed her anger.

'If you'll remember, *I'm* the one who told you about this child, Oliver. I didn't have to. I'm also the one who told the palace, knowing that they'd force me into this.'

He bridled. 'Force you into marrying me? No one's forcing anyone to do anything. I thought we were having fun. That we—'

She cut him off. 'I don't want to marry someone to be a bit of *fun*.'

He could practically see Lia's emotions withdraw like the tide, and in their place came the ice. So why wasn't he throwing a pickaxe into the wall between them and breaking through the ice to that warm, beautiful heart of hers?

She fixed him with her pale blue eyes. 'I didn't want this. *Any* of this.'

The words hung between them like daggers.

Everything they hadn't discussed about the future hovered above them like an enormous wave, about to drown them with the sheer weight of it all. A wave comprised of one question: did they love one another?

He rattled through a checklist of their lives. The positives? Life on St Victoria was amazing. The past month had been wonderful. They each did their jobs without the impediment of their pasts. The negatives? Lia's life wasn't picture-perfect. Until they'd met she'd been isolated.

Lonely. And, when you put a magnifying glass to it, Oliver's life wasn't perfect either. He was caring for everyone but himself. Salving other people's wounds whilst his own remained untended.

Beyond the window he caught a glimpse of the fairy castle. The very turret he'd said he'd climb to tell one and all how he felt about Lia.

But he hadn't.

This conversation, he realised, was what they had to survive before either of them got their happy ending. Their darkest fears had to be confronted.

'What do you want, Lia? What do you really want?' Oliver asked.

'I want to marry someone who wants to marry *me*. Not the palace. Not the baby. Not anything else but me.'

He knew what she was saying. She wanted to marry someone who was in love with her. And of all the people in the world, she deserved nothing less.

He felt the bone-deep ache of knowing he'd approached this from the wrong angle. From the moment he'd found out she was pregnant his focus had been on the baby. He'd been so intent on ensuring he became a father that he hadn't allowed his feelings for Lia the space they deserved.

She'd trusted him.

And, stupidly, he'd broken that precious link.

She spoke before he could. 'I didn't think you had it in you to do something so cruel. But lucky me! Now I know exactly who it is I've agreed to marry, I'm not so certain I think it's a very good idea.'

Washes of hot and cold swept through him so fast he didn't have time to react to either one.

Splitting up when they'd only just begun their journey together was the last thing he wanted, but he wasn't going to insist upon pursuing a marriage she saw as a trap. A cage.

There was only one option.

'All right then.' Oliver looked Lia straight in the eye. 'The wedding's off.'

CHAPTER ELEVEN

OLIVER'S VOICE WAS barely penetrating the roar of blood pounding through her head.

He didn't want to marry her.

She stared at his mouth, trying to parse the words as he spoke.

'Your happiness and the baby's wellbeing are what's important here,' he said.

A complete understanding of the situation cracked open her chest and laid her heart bare. She'd never felt more humiliated. More blind to what had been happening all along. Oliver genuinely didn't want her. He wanted the baby. An heir. A child to replace the one he'd been denied.

Her heart ached for the pain he'd endured, but that was no reason to play such a cruel game with her emotions.

She pulled the ring off her finger, pressed it into Oliver's hand, and fled the room before he could see a single tear fall. She didn't need to listen to the rest of whatever he was going to say before she put his name on the growing list of people who didn't want her.

First her mother, then her father, then a string of so-called friends and boyfriends. They hadn't wanted her. Just something *from* her. Status. Prestige. Their picture in a glossy magazine. Those were the reasons a handful of girls back at school had been friendly towards her. They certainly hadn't actually wanted to be friends.

But wanting her for a baby?

That was a new level of low she couldn't wrap her head around. Nor did it match the man she'd connected with so perfectly that first, undeniably wonderful night. The night they had conceived their child.

She blindly got into the lift, not caring which floor it landed on. What did matter? The one thing she'd thought was a certainty in her life had just been shattered into a million unfixable pieces.

She'd thought the protective shield she'd built around herself was strong enough to endure another assault. A safe haven. But she'd let that shield fall for Oliver. The one man she'd ever let herself truly love. And he only wanted her for the child she was going to bear.

Icy-cold tendrils of darkness swept through her bloodstream and tightened their hold on her heart. She'd thought she'd known loneliness before, but she'd been wrong. *This* was what real loneliness felt like. Bone-crushing loss.

'Lia?'

Lia looked around her. Somehow she'd ended up in front of the hotel.

'What are you doing out here?'

Grace reached out and touched her hand, her eyes dropping to the bare ring finger that was effectively telling the story Lia couldn't yet put a voice to.

Grace's expression sobered—a direct contrast to her theme park tiara and jolly pink and white polka-dotted carry-all. 'You okay?'

No. She was about as far from okay as it got. Not that she could say as much. Especially not to someone she worked with.

Up until a handful of weeks ago, crossing the line between her work and personal lives had been something she'd avoided as if her life depended upon it. Work was the one sanctuary that had never let her down, and merely thinking about letting Grace or anyone else into her private life more than she had terrified her.

'Come, darlin',' Grace said after a moment, her soft island lilt as soothing as her touch. 'Come with me.'

'But…aren't you off to the airport?'

'You can come with us if you want.'

Lia started rummaging round in the tote bag she'd blindly grabbed as she'd left the suite. 'I don't think I have my passport…'

What little self-possession she had began to crumble. There was no way she could go back up there, tail between her legs, and get her passport. Stomping in and out wasn't her style either. Hiding out and reading books and going to work was her style. A desperate longing for her little cottage on St Victoria took hold.

She stiffened when she felt someone else by her side.

'Lia!'

Élodie. Yet another reminder of Oliver.

As Lia did her best to dredge up a smile, the young girl looked up into her face and, with the unerring eye of a child who had known more tragedy than she should have, instantly read the situation.

'Here.' She handed Lia the magic wand Oliver had bought her yesterday. 'I think you might need this more than me.'

Lia made a weird laughing, snuffling, hiccuping noise, then dropped down so that she was at eye level with Élodie. 'Thank you, love, but I don't think even a magic wand can fix things today.'

Élodie looked at her with such disbelief it disarmed her. 'But...' the little girl protested. 'But believing in something hard enough, strong enough, is supposed to make almost every wish come true.'

Lia wanted to refute that. Tell her, no, that wasn't the way the world worked. And then it dawned on her that of all the people in the world Élodie was one of those who knew that every dream didn't come true. No matter how hard she prayed, wished or waved her magic wand, her parents would never come back. Nor would she ever get back one solitary minute of the weeks and weeks of her childhood she'd spent in hospital. She understood what reality was in the deepest possible way, and still she faced the future with hope.

Lia shifted her hand to her belly and forced herself to take a deep breath in and out.

Okay. Things with Oliver might not have gone the way she wanted. In fact, they'd gone completely the opposite way to what she wanted. But she was still pregnant with a little boy or girl who had their entire life in front of them. And she wanted more than anything to make sure that future was a good one.

'I think it's fate we ran into each other,' Grace said gently. 'Please, join us.'

'But…passport…?'

Grace gave her arm a squeeze, then waved her hand. 'I can run up and get that. Not a problem.' She turned to go, then stopped and turned back. 'You know, I'm going to take Élodie to see my daughter and her family when we land. Would you like to come?'

'You have a daughter?'

Grace tried and failed to mask her surprise that Lia didn't know, 'Yes—and a son.'

Lia felt yet another tectonic shift. Not because Grace had children—more because in all of the three years they'd worked together, Lia had never asked her.

Was the cocoon she'd accused Oliver of putting her in actually one she'd made herself? Was the protective shield she'd held up between herself and loneliness actually the reason for it?

'How old is she? Your daughter?'

'Just gone thirty. Given me two lovely grand-babies, she has.'

Lia frowned. How had she not known this?

'My boy is twenty-eight and set to be married next spring... I'm sorry I could go on and on about them,' Grace tacked on in an apologetic tone, 'so I'll stop.'

'No, please. I'm interested.'

Lia felt ashamed. Just because she didn't like people to know about her own life didn't mean she couldn't show an interest in other people's. Grace had been nothing but kind to her through three years, and she hadn't even known she had grown children, let alone grandchildren.

A niggle of discomfort that Oliver might have been right to treat her with kid gloves needled into her conscience. There were a thousand questions she should've been asking him over these past few weeks. About his past, his hopes, his dreams. The same thousand questions he should've been asking her...

'Here's your taxi, ma'am.' A bellhop carrying

a couple of wheelie bags splashed with bright tropical flowers bearing The Island Clinic luggage tags gestured to a car a few metres away.

Grace leant in and in a low voice said, 'Élodie's aunt and uncle are still off working on that yacht job, so I thought I'd take her for a playdate and maybe an overnight stay with my daughter's girls, before she heads back to an empty house.'

'Don't the aunt and uncle have children?'

Grace pulled a face. 'They're all teenagers, fresh out of school, and they're working as well,' she explained with a shake of her head. 'I hate thinking of that poor girl spending so much time on her own… Melody won't mind if I bring one more.'

'Melody?' Lia repeated.

'My daughter,' Grace said, as if Lia should know this. She pushed her lips forward, then shifted her weight to her other hip and stared at Lia—*hard*. She blinked once, her expression unreadable, then said, 'Joining us doesn't obligate you to anything.'

Lia wished she could pull their entire interchange from the air and incinerate it. What *was* it with her? She had to stop pushing people away if she was ever going to get that so-called normal life she wanted.

'No!' she insisted. 'Really. That's not it. Not it at all. I just want to— I want—'

She wanted to be with Oliver. Wanted it to be yesterday, when everything had seemed perfect—like a fairy tale. But life wasn't a fairy tale. It was real. Oliver had just called their wedding off. And she had to take some responsibility for that.

Her new life would have to begin with the smallest of steps. Or, in this case, a plane ride. 'Yes, please, Grace. I'd love to come.'

Grace's face brightened into a broad smile and Élodie jumped up and down, shouting, 'Yippee!'

Grace nodded to the taxi and said to Lia, 'You go on ahead and help Élodie get buckled up. I'll go get your passport.'

When Grace reappeared, she wasn't alone.

Oliver was with her, his expression taut with a determination Lia had never seen before. He was as handsome as ever, and his blue eyes glittered with an inner strength that made him appear both powerful and kind. He'd opened his heart to her, told her of his darkest moment, his biggest fear, and she'd made it about herself. Had unleashed her fears on him like weapons.

The fact that he was here made her respect for him soar up a few more notches. He was a man who faced his problems head-on. She needed to prove she could do the same. If it turned out he didn't love her, they'd find some way to deal with it…to move on. To ensure that Oliver was in her child's life.

Would it break her heart? Absolutely. Would she do it for her child. Without reservation.

She stepped towards him. The air around them was electric with the myriad emotions both of them were feeling.

Her list was pretty long: hope, fear, hurt and, yes, love. Still love.

He wasn't saying anything. It was up to her to break the silence.

'Hey…'

She cringed. There was definitely room for improvement in her truce-making skills.

Eyes glued to hers, Oliver said, 'I understand there's cake on offer at Melody's.'

Lia glanced at Grace, who was looking entirely too innocent for someone who had clearly told Oliver his fiancée was trying to run away.

Ex-fiancée.

Her gut churned. She didn't want to be his ex. She wanted to be his someone. For him to be hers. The one person in the world who knew everything about her. The good, the bad, and everything else in between.

A tiny little bloom of hope rose in her chest.

The fact that he was here meant something, right?

Maybe they'd got it all wrong when they'd fought.

Maybe Oliver was as nervous as she was. Just as full of concerns and anxieties about their future.

They should have started talking about more than their favourite colours and dog breeds the day they'd found out she was pregnant. They should still be talking now.

If only he wasn't so utterly kissable!

Not a good enough excuse.

This wasn't the time to think about how much he loved it when she traced her fingers along his collarbone, or kissed him just under the ridge of his jaw, or slid alongside him, spooning their naked bodies together as if they'd been designed for one another.

She looked up and saw that Oliver was examining her, presumably trying to figure out what she was smiling about when he'd just called off their wedding.

A blush crept into her cheeks.

Jumping on him and ripping his clothes off wasn't the solution. Talking was.

Sensing that things weren't going to turn into sunshine and roses and, more to the point, that there wasn't going to be another proposal here in the taxi rank, Grace bustled everyone into the car, where she and Élodie kept up a flow of conversation about the theme park, and how the Room Service fries were curly, not straight, and how they loved the scent of the lotion in the bathroom at the hotel, but how nice it would be to get back home.

Élodie gravely informed them that she'd reached a few conclusions, including the fact that going to theme parks was extra-fun. Especially with adults, because they laughed more than they did in real life. Also, she was going to join the swim team when she was old enough, because mermaids seemed very special indeed, and finally, living like a princess every day did seem to have *some* plus points, but maybe not every day—because princesses probably couldn't have chocolate cake.

Lia managed to share a smile with Oliver at this. The one thing she'd been craving since she fell pregnant was chocolate cake.

Throughout the ride, the flight, and the second taxi ride to Grace's daughter's house, Lia and Oliver were mostly silent. But the angry tension from their fight had softened—largely thanks to Élodie, who could wrap Oliver round her little finger like a soft piece of ribbon. Which, of course, made Lia love him that little bit more.

When they got to the house they both stayed on the porch, saying they needed a minute before coming in.

'I just have to make a quick call,' they said at the same time.

Their nervous laughs twined together.

'I need to call my father,' she said, at the same time as he told her he needed to call his parents.

'To call things off?' she dared to ask.

Grace shooed Élodie inside before Oliver could answer.

'To clear the air,' Oliver said once they were alone.

Which was interesting. Why would he need to clear the air with his parents?

'Should we maybe do that first? Clear the air?' she asked, hoping he wanted to salvage things as much as she did. 'Before we call home?'

He tipped his head to the side, his eyes glued to her as if he was trying to see her from a different angle. She prayed with every fibre in her being that he saw the hope in her heart.

'Good idea,' he said.

And just like that she could breathe again.

As if by spoken agreement they went in and joined Grace's family, each of them needing just a bit more time to collect their thoughts before they had *that talk*. The one that would decide their future.

Once the little girls had been sorted out with some games, Grace, Lia and Oliver sat on the patio, enjoying the shade over the picnic table as Grace's daughter brought out an enormous chocolate cake.

'Chocolate's supposed to help you fall in love—but I guess you two don't need the extra boost, do you?' Melody smiled at Lia, putting the cake down in front of her.

Lia tried and failed to fight the sting of tears at the back of her throat.

'Oh! Did I say the wrong thing?' Melody's eyes shot to her mother. Grace shook her head.

Oliver cleared his throat and took a long drink of iced tea.

Poor Melody obviously had no idea what was going on, but she innately knew that making a fuss would be a bad idea.

Grace rose and said, 'Melody? I wonder if you wouldn't mind helping me rustle up a few sandwiches for the little ones.'

Lia shot her a grateful smile. She was giving Oliver and Lia some much-needed alone time.

Melody began to head to the kitchen. 'I'm not sure we have any bread…'

'Well, then…' Grace looked positively thrilled by this news. 'I don't think these two will mind if we pop to the store, do you?' She gave Oliver a look. 'If you hear screaming, would you mind looking in on the children?'

Laughing, Melody rolled her eyes. 'We'll take them with us.' She gave her mother a tight, fierce hug. 'I know it's only been forty-eight hours, but it's good to have my best friend back.'

'Your mother, you mean,' Lia corrected, without thinking.

'No...' Melody shook her head. 'She's my mama, but more than that she's my bestie.' She gave her mother a little hip-bump and the two of them shared a complicit cackle, then started rounding up the children.

A deep longing Lia had never acknowledged opened in her chest. A painful, agonising hunger she'd tried to hide for almost her entire life. The hunger for the love and friendship of her mother.

The tears she'd been trying to keep at bay finally began to fall.

Oliver pulled out a fresh handkerchief and handed it to her, then nudged a slice of cake in front of her. 'You know they say a problem shared is a problem halved...'

She let the invitation sit between them, and after a moment's hesitation said, 'Even if we're not getting married any more?'

Oliver drew in a sharp breath, then said, 'Let's not worry about the wedding right now.

What's important is that we understand each other.'

'Well… I guess what we need to talk about is the fact you called off the wedding.'

He held up a hand. 'I did that because it seemed like the last thing on earth you wanted. And I don't want it if you don't want it.'

The way he said it opened up a warm ray of sunshine in her heart. 'So…you still want to marry me?'

He took the ring out of his shirt pocket and put it on the table between them. 'Why don't we have a good long talk and see what we come up with.'

So Lia began to talk. And talk and talk and talk. With an openness and candour she'd never allowed herself before.

She told Oliver about her childhood. Her parents' acrimonious divorce. Her mother's exile when the royal council had insisted Lia and her father move back into the palace to 'keep things in order' once the divorce had been finalised. Her father's emotional withdrawal. Boarding school. Her lack of friends. The pleasure she'd found working in medicine. How it had doubled when she'd begun to do it at The Island Clinic in St Victoria.

'And then I met you.'

Their gazes caught and held, the magic of that night returning with a strength she wouldn't have thought possible.

'And you fell pregnant.'

Lia nodded. 'And the palace said we had to get married.'

'And that made you unhappy?' Oliver asked.

It was a loaded question and they both knew it.

'It frightened me.'

'Why?

Again the sting of tears struck, hard and fast. 'I don't want what happened to my parents to happen to us.'

There. She'd said it. And the world hadn't ended. Oliver hadn't fled for the hills. Quite the opposite, in fact. He was leaning in, taking her hands in his, a sweet, gorgeous, earnest expression on his face.

'We won't let it.'

'How do you know?'

'Because we love each other.'

She blinked away a few tears. 'You've never said that.'

He grimaced. 'I know. I should have. I did. I *do*. I just...' He took a steadying breath. 'I let what happened in the past fine-tune my focus on the baby. *Our* baby. It blinded me to the fact that I was falling in love with you. When you left the hotel room today I suddenly realised just how big a part of my life you've become. Obviously I can't wait to meet our baby, but every single moment I think about having is with you. Without you...' He shook his head. 'I don't want a life without you. We're the ones who are giving this child life and I want us to raise it together—as a family. Bring it on trips to Disney World—every year if you want. Or we can lock the rest of the world out and have it be just the three of us, tucked away in the treehouse. Or even living in separate houses—'

'No.' She shook her head, laughing now. 'Not separate houses.' She put her hand on his heart, gratified to feel it pounding as quickly as her own. 'I think I was scared to admit it too. That I loved you. And even now that I know I do, it feels like giving up part of myself. My control.'

He nodded. 'Given your past, I'm not surprised. It seems as if everyone you've let yourself love has disappointed you in some way. I don't want to be one of those people.'

She touched his cheek, speechless. It felt as if they were practically exchanging vows here and now.

She picked the ring up from the table and held it between them. 'What if I were to put this on again and promise never to take it off?'

Relief flooded Oliver's chest. Lia still wanted to marry him. 'You'd be making me a very happy man.'

Lia handed him the ring and, as if they were at the ceremony itself, he slipped it onto her finger.

'Feel good?' he asked.

'It feels perfect.' She looked across at him. 'You know, I've done a lot of pouring my heart out…are there any problems you'd like halved?'

He laughed, his fingers toying with the ring on Lia's finger. 'You don't want the wedding at the palace, do you?'

She shook her head. 'No, I don't. I want it here on St Victoria. On a date we want, with guests we want and the food we want. Chocolate cake, obviously. On the beach.' Quickly she added, 'If that's what you want?'

'It sounds perfect.' He dropped a kiss onto the back of her hand. 'Especially if we throw in a midnight swim after the guests have gone.'

She grinned, but her smile faded as, once again, reality surfaced. 'I don't quite know how we're going to derail all the palace plans...'

'I have an idea,' Oliver said. 'Rather than make phone calls, why don't we get on planes? To Europe? You and I still have loads to talk about, and by the time we land in England I think we'll have a pretty good game plan.'

'For what?' Lia gave him a sidelong glance.

'For letting our parents know we're our own people now. That we love them, we respect them, but that our futures are precisely that. *Ours.*'

Three days later, Lia felt as if she had literally entered another world. A world preserved in time every bit as much as her own childhood had been.

'Ready?' Oliver asked, giving her hand a squeeze.

'As I'll ever be,' she said, lifting a pair of crossed fingers, which Oliver kissed for extra luck.

Huge stone lions stood atop enormous granite pillars at the top of an avenue of trees that had clearly seen generations of Bainbridges make their way to the family seat.

Summer was in its full glory in England, and the Bainbridges' estate was no different.

'I see Mother's made sure the flowers are all in full bloom for you.'

Lia gave him a funny look, because she hadn't seen anything, and then, as they passed down the final length of the tree-lined avenue she gasped in delight. In front of them was an enormous country house…palace? Whatever it was, it was impressive. A sprawl of windows and climbing roses and balconies and turrets was buttressed by immaculately manicured gardens. There was a huge lake off to one side, along with another smaller but far from small house. And beyond that another.

'The Dowager Duchess's house. Currently empty,' Oliver explained. 'And those are the stables, off to the left. Mostly empty too, I suppose, apart from my parents' horses.'

'And you're sure about your idea? The one you want to put to your parents?' she asked.

'Look at the place,' he said, steering the car with a practised hand into the large circular drive. 'It's enormous. No amount of children we have could ever fill it.'

'Good point.' She laughed, her nerves getting the better of her.

His parents' place—Oliver's birthright—was every bit as grand as the palace she'd grown up in. She leant forward, trying to absorb the splendour of it all, then suddenly, thinking of their lives back in St Victoria, started properly giggling.

'What?'

'You grew up in a stately home and now you live in a treehouse!' She hooted.

Oliver feigned deep hurt. 'I thought you liked my treehouse!'

'I love it more than ever,' she said, meaning it. 'You do realise you grew up in a costume drama, right?'

Oliver laughed. 'It was a drama, all right.' He sighed, his shoulders slumping. 'Cold War more like.'

Amelia turned in her seat to face him. 'Oli…

Are you okay? You don't have to do this, you know.'

'I do,' he assured her, giving her a quick smile before pulling the car up in front of the house. 'Besides, I've got my superpower now.'

'What superpower is that?' Lia asked, thinking of the multitude he already possessed.

'You.'

It took the arrival of a butler to stop the kissing that ensued. Holding hands, red-faced and still giggling, Lia and Oliver went up the grand entrance steps to meet his parents.

An hour later Oliver wondered who had kidnapped his parents and replaced them with the kind, interested couple sitting before him.

Gone were the icy exteriors, the uncomfortable handshakes and awkward chit-chat about the weather. In their place were welcoming greetings, enthusiastic storytelling—mostly embarrassing stories from Oliver's childhood—and a warmth he'd never once experienced in their company.

They were sitting underneath a loggia draped in frothy purple and white wisteria blossoms, eating a rather impressive afternoon tea. The nerves that had been jack-knifing round Oliver's ribcage reached critical mass. It was now or never time.

He felt the weight of his parents' eyes shifting to him. His mother's. His father's. His bewitching bride-to-be's. He drew his strength from her—and her nod of encouragement.

After he'd explained his idea to his parents, he sat back in his chair. 'If you'd like some time to think about it, please do.'

His parents looked at one another, silently exchanging information, and then, as one, gave each other a nod of understanding.

In that instant Oliver understood a thousand things about them that he'd never understood before. They loved one another. Very deeply. They just loved one another in their own way. Now that he was grown, and the stress of parenting had been taken out of their hands, they were able to relax into the lives they had wanted to live all along. Whereas he loved interacting with children, they loved interacting with adults. They loved old—he loved whimsical.

They loved him. They simply hadn't known how to love him as a child.

That revelation cleared the way for an entirely

new relationship with them. He swallowed, his heart lodging in his throat. A relationship he might have just compromised with his proposal.

'We love it,' his father said. 'There will be the particulars to organise, of course. One doesn't simply snap one's fingers to change a house like this into an activity centre for underprivileged children, but…yes… I like it.' He turned to Lia. 'The old place has done its time serving the country before, you know.'

'Oh…?'

'During World War I. I hadn't even been born then, but I've seen the pictures. My father, and his father before him, cleared every room in the place and turned it into a hospital for returning soldiers. Wretched business they'd been through, poor chaps.' He stopped and gave his chin a thoughtful rub, turned to Oliver. 'These young ones you're proposing to move in…do you suppose they'd mind a couple of oldies knocking around the place? The estate, I mean?'

'Absolutely not! I didn't mean it needed to become an activity centre straight away. This is your home. You do with it exactly what you want, as long as you want to.'

Oliver gave himself an invisible thump on the head and went on to explain that he'd meant in a few years' time. He and Lia were perfectly happy in St Victoria, and didn't plan on moving back to the UK even when the estate was transformed into an activity centre for underprivileged children. They'd come back, of course. Frequently. But…

'I love you both,' he said. 'But this is how we see ourselves being involved in the estate in the future. I can't do what you did—uphold all those traditions. I'll try my very best to honour them, but we want to live our lives differently. We don't want the wedding in Karolinska. We don't want to live on a huge estate. We're doctors, and in a few months we'll be parents. That's where we want our focus to be.'

'Oliver.'

His mother gave him a look he remembered all too well from his childhood. The *Children should be seen and not heard* look.

He nodded for her to go ahead, grateful for the warmth of Lia's touch as she reached out to take one of his hands in hers. They shared a smile, and any nerves he'd felt slipped away. She loved his idea about the activity centre and had said she'd do everything in her power to support him. Holding his hand in plain view of his mother's stern gaze was all the proof he needed that she meant it.

'Oliver,' his mother repeated. 'Your father and I only live in a few of the rooms here, and we have actually been eyeing up the Dowager's house as alternative accommodation. We needed a bit of a push to get that particular ball rolling and you have now done it. If you would like to turn the estate into this activity place next week, you may...'

She paused and cleared her throat a couple of times, then paused again to clear what Oliver suddenly realised was an unexpected rush of emotion.

She looked at him with her clear blue eyes and said, 'Your father and I would be very pleased...very *proud*...if you were to go ahead with your plans whenever you like. In fact...' She looked at her husband. 'Why wait? From this very moment it's yours. Consider it an early wedding gift.'

Lia choked on her tea. 'What?'

'Brilliant idea. Wonderful. Yes. The estate is yours.' Oliver's father gave his wife's hand a pat as he spoke, his eyes shifting from Lia to Oliver. 'We didn't give you much of a child-hood, son, but we are very, very proud of the man you've become. And if turning this old echoey lump of stone into a house full of children properly enjoying themselves means we'll get to see more of you, the least we can do is start the ball rolling immediately.'

Too choked up to speak, Oliver rose—and for the first time in his life hugged his father.

Lia held her father's hands in her own. Their reunion had been trickier, but no less fruitful. 'And you're absolutely positive you're happy to tell Grandmama and Grandpapa?'

Behind her father, Oliver gave her a double thumbs-up.

She'd done it. She'd told him she didn't want to have the wedding at the palace and that, more than anything, she and Oliver wanted a simple beach wedding, with no press. But, if he was happy to come, she would love him to walk her down the aisle.

'I will tell them tonight.'

Lia winced. 'We're going to be on a plane tonight.'

'I know.'

Her father gave her a wicked grin she hadn't seen for decades—one that spoke of the little boy he'd once been. The one who'd used to learn magic tricks and do puppet shows in the nursery for the palace staff.

'I thought you might like to be a few thousand miles away in case your grandmother screams in protest.'

Lia laughed. 'Should we get you some ear plugs before we go?'

'I think I can handle it,' her father said, his smile fading a bit as their eyes met again. 'Watching this palace empty of young people has taught me something.'

'What's that?'

'That we need to change. *I* need to change. A royal family that no one wants to be in isn't much of an example to the nation, is it?'

The knot of emotion in Lia's chest softened. 'Dad…' she began, her voice less tentative than it had been when she'd told him she didn't want to be married in Karolinska. 'Do you think…do you think Mum could be persuaded to come?'

He shook his head. 'I don't know, love. But

if there's anything I can do to help you get her on a plane, I will.'

Lia looked at him and saw that age-old flame he'd held for her mother was still burning bright. She gave him a hug, love pouring through her when she felt his hands close around her back to return the embrace. She would reach out to her mother. If she came, great. If not...perhaps she'd come when the baby was born.

In the car on the way back to the airport she leant back and breathed a sigh of relief.

'Happy?' Oliver asked.

'Mostly,' she said, leaning in to snuggle close to him, her cheek on his shoulder, their hands intertwined.

The reunion hadn't been as horrible as she'd thought it might be. Nor had it been quite as celebratory as Oliver's had. But that was okay, because she knew now, no matter what, that she would have the man she loved by her side from here on out. He was here for her, for her child, and for the family they would become. And that was what mattered most.

CHAPTER TWELVE

ÉLODIE ACCEPTED THE vibrant crown of tropical flowers as a queen might accept a tiara weighted with a nation's finest jewels.

'What do you think?' Lia asked as she turned the little girl around so that she faced the mirror.

Élodie grinned at herself, then up at Lia, who had opted for a solitary white blossom tucked behind her ear. 'I think that you look like a mermaid, and that I look like a princess, and that I'm pretty sure I want to live in a treehouse when I grow up!'

Lia laughed, and then, realising Élodie was speaking of so much more than a roof over her head, pulled her in for a hug, tight enough so that she wouldn't see the tears in her eyes. She felt for the girl and, even though she knew she had their own child growing in her belly, she wondered if Oliver would agree to one last pre-wedding request.

After sending Élodie out to find 'Granny Bainbridge', as Oliver's mother had come to be known, she went to the guest room, where Oliver was getting ready. 'Knock-knock!'

Oliver jumped behind the door so she couldn't see him. 'I thought it was bad luck to see one another before the ceremony.'

Lia laughed, stupidly pleased that Oliver was such a lovely mix of tradition and quirky uniqueness. She was a lucky woman.

She pressed her hands to the door, imagining his face as she asked her question. 'Oli...?'

'Yes, my love?'

'How would you feel about expanding our family by one more?'

His head popped out from the other side of the door. 'What? You're already pregnant! You can't— Are you—?' Lines fanned out from his beautiful blue eyes as the wheels of his mind whirred to try and make sense of what she'd just asked. 'What's going on? Help a man on his wedding day, my darling bride.'

She grinned at him, unable to resist ruffling his tidy blond hair with her hand. 'What medical school did you go to? It's rare, but you can actually be pregnant with two babies at one time. It's called superfetation.'

His eyes widened. 'It's only been a few weeks. You know already?'

Lia laughed. Their sex life was definitely active enough to have produced another child—but, no. As she'd said, superfetation was an extremely rare occurrence, and that wasn't what she had in mind.

She patted her tummy. 'Just the one baby for now. I was actually thinking of...' She bit down on her lip, her eyes drifting out to the beach, where Élodie was trying to coax Oliver's mother to dip her bare toes into the surf, squealing as the water hit her feet and splashed her shins.

Oliver's eyes snapped back to hers as he finally connected the dots. 'You want to adopt Élodie?'

She raised her eyebrows, sank her teeth deeper into her lip. Until she'd asked it, she hadn't realised just how much she wanted Élodie to be a part of their everyday lives.

Oliver's face broke into a broad smile. Before she could talk to him about speaking with Élodie's aunt and uncle, and of course the adoption authorities, or say anything practical at all, Oliver had her in his arms and was swinging her round and round, whooping as if she'd just agreed to marry him all over again.

'What's going on up there?' Lia's father called from the beach, where he'd been walking with Oliver's father. 'It sounds as if you're being attacked by a tribe of wild monkeys!'

'Not quite,' Lia called from the balcony. 'We'll be down in a minute. Is everyone ready for the wedding?'

A collective cheer went up from the beach where, in the end, quite a few more friends and family than they'd originally planned to invite had gathered for their small, informal wedding.

Guests had been asked to leave their mobile phones and cameras at home—not out of a strict 'no photos' rule, but out of a desire for them to be present in the moment as Lia and Oliver exchanged their vows. Marriage wasn't just about the two of them. It was about everyone they cared for and everyone who cared for them.

Ten minutes later, her arm tucked into the crook of her father's, Lia was walking down the 'aisle'—a petal path that Élodie was making as she skipped ahead of Lia, fistfuls of flowers floating in her wake. She saw Oliver's parents. Her own parents exchanging surprisingly flirtatious glances. Her cousin. Friends from the clinic. Grace…

The King and Queen of Karolinska had opted out of the wedding, saying something about the tropical heat not suiting their constitutions, but they had invited Oliver and Lia to join them at their summer retreat at the end of the month, for a less formal chance to get to know one another.

Lia's eyes eventually met and locked with Oliver's. This was the man whose smile she knew she would look forward to seeing every day of her life. Today it held an additional secret, of course. The knowledge that they would, once they'd spoken to the appropriate people, invite Élodie to join their small, growing family.

Lia glanced back at the treehouse, easily imagining it filled with the sound of children's laughter, and her heart felt fit to burst.

When their celebrant finished his introductory remarks and began the ceremony, Lia's heart launched into her throat as Oliver's voice grew thick with emotion as he began to recite his vows.

'I seek to know you.' Oliver's eyes briefly met Lia's, his voice catching in his throat as he continued. 'For all the years to come I will take joy in you. I will endeavour to see you as you are and love you for all that is familiar and for all of your mysteries.'

As he spoke, his words so pure in intention, she could hardly believe everything that was happening was real. It was the world's largest *pinch me* moment.

'Amelia? Do you accept Oliver's vows to you?' the celebrant prompted, and their friends and family gave an appreciative laugh. They knew a nervous woman when they saw one.

Lia started. She had been so busy staring into Oliver's eyes, gazing at his mouth, enjoying the sound of his voice, she'd not even noticed he'd stopped speaking.

'Yes!' she cried, and then more gently, as Oliver took her hands in his and her hammering heart calmed itself, 'Yes. I do accept them.' She shifted her dress, the billows of diaphanous blue and green dip-dyed fabric catching in the breeze. 'And with all my heart I will honour them as I hope he will honour mine.'

Oliver said, 'I will!'

Lia laughed along with the crowd. 'You haven't even heard them yet.'

Oliver's face tightened with emotion for the briefest of moments before clearing. His expression told her everything she'd ever wanted to know about him. He loved her and would do anything for her. There might be ups and downs, and he might not get it right the first time, but he'd keep on trying. No matter what, he'd keep on trying until he got it right.

Wiping away a few happy tears, she began, 'Oliver Bainbridge, from the moment I met you I knew in my heart I'd met a kindred spirit. Someone whose word is his passion. Whose passions make his life and the lives of those around him richer, kinder, better. I will respect and honour our friendship, our romantic love, and the path we choose as parents. I will also respect and honour the path you choose as the man who has asked me to walk hand in hand with him throughout this amazing, crazy life we're about to live. It's only just begun, and already I can't wait to grow old with you and love you more with each passing day. I love you. I respect you. And I am truly the proudest woman in the world that you are about to be my husband and the father to our children.'

Before the celebrant could ask Oliver if he would honour and respect Lia's vows to him Oliver was kissing her. It was a fiery, possessive, hungry, happy kiss, and Lia felt every molecule of her body become supercharged when, through it all, she heard the celebrant announce them as husband and wife.

'I would now like to introduce to you Their Royal Highnesses the Doctors Bainbridge!'

As they walked past their friends and family, everyone's faces beaming with shared joy, Oliver and Lia exchanged a secret smile. They knew everyone would be expecting them to head up to the massive buffet, spread out beneath the canopy of tropical trees, but there was just one more thing they wanted to do before they were well and truly married.

Oliver gave Lia's hand a squeeze. 'You sure you're all right with getting your beautiful dress wet?'

'More than.'

And with that they ran into the sea, hand

in hand, emerging wet, glistening in the sun and beaming at one another, more certain than they'd ever been that the future would be a much better place because they were together.

* * * * *

LET'S TALK

Romance

For exclusive extracts, competitions
and special offers, find us online:

f facebook.com/millsandboon

⊙ @millsandboonuk

🐦 @millsandboon

Or get in touch on 0844 844 1351*

For all the latest titles coming soon,
visit millsandboon.co.uk/nextmonth